The Midnight Murders
By Ashley Evans

Many thanks to Megan, for giving me the encouragement, inspiration and passion, to write this novel, and for the cover art of this novel.

Chapter One
The Beginning Of The Nightmare

The cold, spread like a disease, over the pitch black engulfed forest of Clapham Woods, near Worthing, West Sussex. The breeze, gently brushing the leaves, bushes and grass in the endless maze of wood. Clapham Woods had a reputation for being haunted. Several pets, mostly dogs, and people, have gone missing there since the 1970s. However, alarmingly, some people had been found in the woods. Dead. Tonight, September 21st 2018, was no different. The usually quiet and lonely woods were crawling with police officers, forensics and detectives. One such detective, DI Greg Cowper, was not used to death. This was to be his first case. Marching with an officer deeper and deeper into the forest, Cowper was finally brought to the scene. Blood. Blood, splattered everywhere. Onto the grass, the leaves, the trees. However, no sign of a body. Cowper saw a tall and almost intimidating looking figure, branded a silhouette by the lights attempt at brightening up the scene of the crime. The figure was wearing a black and battered trench coat, hands in pockets. The figure turned, to reveal an unshaven, lethargic face. Ominous clouds underneath his eyes pulled the skin down. With pretty long hair, he

swept it out of his concerned, yet emotionless, face. It was DI James Heller. Sussex Police's finest detective, one of the top in the country. Cowper, on the other hand, was clean shaven, clean cut and pretty dapper for his young age. He defined inexperienced. He gulped, as Heller nodded at the officer, who then left the scene. Heller walked up to a now calming Cowper.
"DI James Heller. What a bloody miserable evening." Heller shook Cowper's hand.
"Nice pun sir. DI Greg Cowper, pleased to meet you." Cowper then glanced past Heller, to see the body. Naked, it was a young woman. The body was covered in stab wounds. The arms and limbs were flayed, with the left leg so much so, that the bone could be seen. Flesh had been carelessly tossed aside, along with dark red insides. The neck, stabbed and slit deep, fresh blood still slowly oozing out. The face, with one slice mark diagonally down the face. The eyes remained slightly open, but glanced at the night sky, lifelessly.
Cowper inhaled. "So… That's our murder victim eh?"
"No no, just one of the forensics playing a prank on us. But yeah, yeah. Have no idea who she is. A group of teens, ghost hunting, found her. They heard someone running away as they got closer…" Heller turned to observe the body, which was being photographed by forensics. "Looks as if our killer was disturbed."
"Fucking hell, so he didn't finish *this*?"
Heller shook his head. Cowper could tell that this was the most serious thing Heller, in his twenty-year career, had ever seen. "Looks to me, like a serial killer looming." Heller frowned, curious. "What makes you think that? I mean I agree, but I'm just curious."

"Well, it's pretty rare to get such a brutal, one off kinda murder I'm guessing."

Heller nodded with a smile at Cowper. "Very good Greg. I mean we could be fucking wrong! But I agree. Looks like we may well do, and if they're this fucked up to do something like this, I'd say we're expecting a taunting letter or something."

Heller and Cowper continued to observe the body, both unnerved.

"Both of us, will go to the autopsy, Worthing Hospital. In the meantime, I have something interesting to show you…" and with that, Heller lead Cowper a few metres behind the body. Heller shone his torch onto the muddy and mushy leaves on the ground. Cowper simply watched on, confused. He peered up at Heller, waiting for an explanation.

Heller analysed the scene. "Some of the leaves, are almost crushed. Way lower down into the ground than the others. Further supports the idea that the killer was disturbed. If he was properly planned, he'd make sure not to leave this trail for us. But because he *was* he didn't have the time to. Looks as if they lead out of the forest perhaps."

Heller shone the torch further into the forest, where more flattened leaves appeared. A short while later, Heller and Cowper were at the fringe of the woods, with two fellow officers. On the tarmacked motorway, a few more leaves remained almost glued to the ground, where muddy footprints were seen getting fainter and fainter on the A27, heading back in the direction of Worthing, before disappearing entirely.

"Escape route." Cowper concluded.

One of the police officers then turned to the two detectives. "Further along the motorway sir, two muddy trainers were found in the dual carriageway. Filled to the brim with mud on the bottom. They've been bagged."
Heller nodded. "Thank you, Sergeant. Well, maybe he is planned, even when the original plan gets fucked up. I'd say our killer had a backpack with him, to change footwear. Throw us off. Well, it may work."
"Unless we have witnesses, and cameras."
"Speed cameras, yeah James. We'll try and find out what we can, I have PC Knight onto that already. If we have any images, we have a rough, early image of the killer. Even without, they'd certainly have a bag, I'm sure of it." Heller lit a cigarette.
"Exactly, I mean there must have been more weapons than a knife to perform *that*! Keep them in the bag with a change of trainers, maybe even a change of clothes. Get changed somewhere before actually getting back to wherever, to confuse us even more." Cowper pointed back into the darkened woods.
Heller's fag sizzled, disturbing the otherwise quiet surroundings. With a puff of smoke, he decided "We need to get this out immediately, get as many leads as possible. I want the whole of Clapham searched." and throwing his fag into the road, Heller turned and headed back in silence into the woods. As he passed the endless bushes and trees, a sound halted him in his tracks. It was paper, blowing gently in the wind. Scanning, quickly, Heller saw an envelope attached to the bark of a tree. "Cowper!" he yelled out as he picked it up, and opened it. Cowper hurried over, to see Heller open the envelope. A polaroid photo of the victim, with less injuries, slipped

out. Cowper picked it up. "It's legitimate then, nobody else could get this. It's a polaroid."

Heller inhaled, and handed Cowper the letter. It read:

```
"To Sussex Police,

Well well well, I think she had a lot
of guts to willingly come to Clapham
Woods with me.
Deadly serious, this is. You see, I'm
bored. I guess that's my motive.
However, unfortunately for you, I am
the definition of elusive. I'm not a
man of many words, so I'll keep it
brief. But I thought I'd attach a
detailed photograph of her, I just
love capturing memories with my
polaroid, you know… The vintage, retro
feel. I disappeared as easily as I
appeared, and I shall continue to do
the same, until you catch me that is.
But if I don't want to be caught, then
I won't be. The fun is only just
starting. It's tempting to butcher
another, just as I become accustomed
to my modus operandi, but you'll have
to wait a little longer. Pulling all
your strings really will have me in
fits.

Kind regards,
```

The Midnight Murderer."

"Well, that's definite confirmation for a serial killer on our hands…" Heller said, with total seriousness.
"Then we'll have to make sure we can grasp him in our hands before anymore murders." Cowper concluded.

By daybreak, the public and country media had gathered in a large group at the police cordon on the A27. The entire woods sat on the bright green grass, like a depressing lump just thrown there. The group chirped away like a rally of insects, all waiting for DI Heller. However, Heller on the other hand, was at Worthing Police Station, which was practically surrounded by an even larger group of press and public. The station had two floors from the outside, a small but almost welcoming looking place. However, the lower two floors were not so much of a welcoming site, often having the pleasure of seeing many come and go from cells. This morning, most were very much vacant. It was Heller's intention to change that. In his office, it stank of coffee. The room had a good view of the street outside, from the second floor of the building, but was scattered with paper and documents, as if thrown everywhere by a toddler with his toys. Heller sat, hunched over, at the desk. He scanned the letter, constantly, in his own little bubble, until a thundering knock at the door burst that bubble. Heller glanced slowly up, to see the young PC Ralph Knight at the door. Knight had a whiny voice, and usually tried to be better than anyone else at the station.

"Prick", Heller always thought whenever he saw him. He inhaled. "Yes Ralph?"

"The correct way to address me is PC Knight, sir."

"Well, I'm not a very correct person. What'd you want?"

Knight gritted his teeth together behind his lipless mouth, before shaking it off and walking up to the desk. Knight looked in distaste at the office.

"Those CCTV tapes you asked for, got 'em." Knight threw a VHS tape onto the desk, causing an avalanche of papers, making Knight raise his eyebrows.

"Oh, and somebody's just come in, saying they have useful information for us concerning the Powell Case."

"Thank you, cunt-stable Knight, thank you very much!" a gleaming Heller, full of jest, then had one final gulp of his coffee, with Knight holding back, before Heller got to his feet and left his office. Knight looked around the unkempt office.

"One day… One day." he sounded like a child in a pathetic strop.

In the main corridor below the office, Jeffrey Stevens sat waiting. The hallway, integrated into the reception, was filled with echoes of officers and police staff, phones constantly ringing on and on and on… A typical Friday morning for the station. Stevens looked tired and miserable, but was not at all impatient. He had a brown, dark haired moustache, and nearly complete enveloping stubble taking over his young face. Heller then walked into the area, where Stevens recognized him instantly and bolted to his feet.

"Jeffrey Stevens yes?"

"Yes sir. I have some pretty damn useful information. About that girl, Jessica Powell." Stevens answered, before yawning. "Excuse me, sorry. Long night."
"Nothing we're not all used to mate, come along with me."
Heller lead Stevens down the long narrow, dark blue walled corridor, before passing a corner sharply. Cowper bumped into Heller.
"Oh, James. Got a useful lead here apparently."
"As have I." Cowper smiled smugly, leaving an also smiling Heller.
"My lead's better than yours'. Oh, right… Erm. Where is yours exactly?" and with a final smug grin, Heller opened the door to an interview room, holding his arm out for Stevens who went inside, followed by Heller and a light slam of the door. Cowper sighed as he hurried up out of the corridor.

Stevens cracked his back as he sat down in a chair. The interview room was dark and freezing. Heller sat down with a groan.
"Fucking Antarctic in here, I do apologise."
"No, not at all!" Stevens was friendly and calm. Heller then flicked the recording tape. After nearly an entire monologue about the details of the room, and who was inside, Stevens began.
"Well, around 11:30PM yesterday, Thursday 20th, I was driving up the A27. Just outside of Worthing, you know, the Durrington sort of area."
Heller nodded.

"Well, just past Findon, I stopped because there was a car in front of me. I thought something was up, but I quickly realised there wasn't. There was a woman, Jessica Powell, beside this VW in front of me, white Tiguan I think. Something like that."

"And, what was Powell doing? Talking to the driver?"

"Yes, she was."

"Any indication of arguments or anything like that?"

"No, to be honest, I thought she was a prozzie or something, by the way she was leaning on this bloke's car, and the way she was dressed."

"Can you remember what she was wearing? We believe the killer took her clothes."

"Short skirt, fishnets and a leather jacket I think."

Heller nodded, also taking every single note, with Stevens watching on like a curious child. "Okay. What did you do next?"

"I stayed for a few seconds. As I said, I thought there was something up. She turned around to look at me. I then just drove off, past the car. Inside, was a hooded man. Black hoodie, that's all. All I saw was stubble, a lot of it. That's it. Then I just drove off, back towards Goring."

"Mr. Stevens, Goring isn't up towards Clapham, or indeed Findon…?"

"Not if you take Long Furlong."

"Yeah, I realise that. But, why take Long Furlong if you left Worthing? It's quicker to get to Goring through Worthing…"

"I know. But I prefer long drives, that's all. I've had a lot of shit at the moment, so getting quiet drives before I get home gives me the isolation I need."

Heller frowned, still taking notes. "We've just had the autopsy report. Did it look as if she was drunk? Or under the influence?"

"She was almost sliding against the car, so I'd guess so yes."

Heller watched the calm and laid-back Stevens. Very, very carefully. In his mind, everyone was a suspect.

The common room, essentially where all the members of the investigation gather round. A large chalk board was covered with a map, photos of the body and the victim alive, with additional notes, Heller wrote up next to large thick bullet points. Every officer watched carefully, with Cowper beside holding onto his folders. Heller took several moments to write up, with the sound of the chalk hitting the board filling the silent room with echoes. He then stopped, and read out the bullet points very firmly. "So, our killer was wearing a black hoodie. Had stubble, from what Jeffrey Stevens saw. He also was driving a white VW, most likely a Tiguan. Powell and the driver were simply talking, she was most likely hitching a ride from the driver. This driver is our killer, okay? The priority right now, is to find that damn car."

Knight's boasting little voice then shouted out. "Since uniform haven't found the car yet sir, we must presume that something has been done with it. Also since the killer walked away from the scene."

All officers turned in sync to stare down at Knight, all wanting to deliberately make him shut up. He sank a little lower into his seat.

"Thank you, our little Knight in shining armour. This is true, but that will not deter us from searching, obviously. Something calculated has happened to it. Now then, hop to it guys."

And with that, all the officers, chatting away, eventually left the common room. Cowper then walked up to Heller, exhaling in impatience, eyebrows raised. Heller took several large gulps from his steaming mug of coffee, before noticing Cowper.

"Oh, shit yeah. You had a lead?"

"At last… Two women have come forward, from a pub called The Black Horse, somewhere in the Durrington/Goring area. Apparently, a known thug I suppose you can call him was previously in a relationship with Powell."

"And who is he?"

"Robert Hall."

Silence. Heller inhaled. "Yes, yes. We all know of him. Woman beater, drug dealer, drug addict… But murderer? Anything else you got?"

Cowper smiled like an excited child. "Uh-huh. When Hall ended the relationship, she started threatening him, blackmailing him in fact. She said she'd go to the police and tell them where his latest stash of drugs are, and trust me, if it's Hall, it's gonna be a shit loada drugs. Anyway, about two weeks ago, at the pub, he started shouting out that he wanted to kill Powell. Now that may just be a drunken outburst, but given his background…"

Heller nodded.

"For that outburst though, we have those two women…" Cowper handed Heller papers regarding the witnesses. "And a certain Mark Hobbes." before handing a final

sheet of paper, which Heller scanned through very quickly.
"Well, we're gonna need more on him. But I think we have a likely suspect Cowper!"
Cowper nodded, with that childlike smile once again, along with Heller sharing the smile before having one final swig of his coffee.

Findon Valley, a small and undisturbed village, literally just one minute out of Durrington. Quiet was the definition of the village, with only a few streets and houses. But, it was close to Clapham Woods, very close. It was distant from its surroundings, however, with the imposing South Downs looking down upon the little place with dominance and very little regard to the tiny village. The village was experiencing mild police activity, but even the police barely took any notice to the village. Surrounding it was the endless A27, along with tall, stretching hills of the South Downs. Standing alone in an uphill road, next to opulent looking houses, was a white VW Tiguan. Passing into the road, two police officers, spotted the vehicle. They turned to each other, briefly confirming between them, before one of them took out his radio. The other, walking up to the car, looked inside. In the back seats laid a coat. Just visible on the North Face hoodie, was blood, desperately trying to be spotted. It wasn't long before Heller and Cowper were at the scene, where the coat was now ready to be examined. Wearing clear white gloves, Heller was passed the thick coat by a forensics officer. He and Cowper briefly examined it, before Heller unzipped the jacket.

"Best to find out who's it is, eh?" Heller instantly found an old name label, and the name shocked him.

Cowper noticed. "What is it?"

Heller inhaled, turning to face Cowper. He then held the coat out, as if on display to be sold. "This coat belongs to Robert Hall."

Chapter Two
Developments

Heller was totally engrossed in several documents about Robert Hall, as he stood next to the car. At the police cordon, on either side, nosy villagers attempted to invade the crime scene but were held back by PCs and PCSOs. Heller took a brief glance at the mugshot of Hall, clipped onto the upper right corner of the papers. A short, stocky man, Hall nevertheless looked merciless. Balding, middle aged, but he simply had a dodgy feel to him. Cowper walked hurriedly over to Heller, along with a small, middle aged man, who was looking impatient and vexed. His white hair blew gently in the breeze, which was clearly annoying him.

"Heller, this is DI Nicholas Hollis." Cowper cleared his throat awkwardly.

"Yes, yes. Morning…" Heller was clearly more interested in the papers, not even looking at Hollis.

Hollis exhaled, very obviously. "Are you just going to be wasting my time Inspector?"

Cowper intervened.

"Hollis is investigating a car theft case, and the car stolen was a white Volkswagen Tiguan. With the same number plates."

Heller instantly threw the papers into his coat, his attention now distracted to Hollis.

"Oh! Right, I see. I bet your glad we solved your case then!"

"No." was the miserable reply from Hollis. "Well, I'd best get this out of the bloody way then. Mr. Elliot White, 34 from Worthing, had his car stolen three days ago from a petrol station."

"Crime of opportunity?" Heller took off his glasses, having finished reading earlier.

"I don't see what that has to do with you."

"Well Inspector, our murderer wouldn't associate himself with the hassle of taking time and effort to steal a car if he's planning to commit murder now, would he?"

Hollis cowered his head, embarrassed that a younger detective would instantly make the assumption.

"Yes, it was a crime of opportunity. Coincidentally, this petrol station had no working CCTV cameras, so we literally have no description of the thief. But what we do have, and my department have emailed this to you, is footage of the car driving from the town centre to here, with different number plates. So, crime of opportunity maybe, but your killer planned an opportunity, so to speak."

Heller simply nodded. "And did you see the driver?"

"Yes. He took off the fake number plates at 3:00AM this morning, a few streets away, and he wore a plain black hoodie."

Mark Hobbes, the exact example of dishevelled. Despite this, he was rather attractive in a rugged way. He was almost Heller but 20 years younger. A busy life, Hobbes rarely got time to relax, but finally he was doing just that.

He sat, in silence, alone. Well, in his own bubble of silence. Hobbes was watching the morning TV in his seemingly empty living room. A twenty something who didn't get a lot of money for their living, wouldn't have their house filled. Nevertheless, the cream coloured living room felt convivial for his needs. His phone vibrated, slowly but surely grabbing his attention. He simply looked at the phone for a split second before turning back to look at the TV. But, a sudden realisation dawned over the distant Hobbes. He then turned back and briskly grabbed his phone. The number was not a saved contact, but the text was to change Hobbes' life forever.

'Don't think about going to the police again Mark, I know where you live. Nah, I'm not smart, I just saw it on your website. But you'll end up like Powell if you utter even one single breath to the police.
With regards,
The Midnight Murderer'

Hobbes felt cold. He felt isolated. He felt scared. The previous, carefree character of Hobbes had been cruelly stolen. Heavy breathing and flooding with sweat, the panicked Mark shakily closed shut the living room curtains of his flat. Throwing his phone to the floor, Mark backed away from it, not baring to even look at it. Hobbes was now, to become, a plaything.

September 23rd, and Heller was for once fresh and full of energy early in the morning. Daybreak fought through the cloudy, overcast skies of Worthing. Heller stood outside the station, waiting for Cowper. Soon enough, Cowper turned around the corner to see the beaming Heller. Confused, he approached Heller with the cautiousness of a hunter.
"What is it? Why you smiling like that?"
"*We* have officially been given a warrant to arrest Robert Hall from the Superintendent." Heller puffed on his fag.
"Shut your ass!" Cowper was gobsmacked.
Heller nodded. "Mmm-hmm. And Hall usually goes to the same old pub, every night, at seven. We'll wait till then to make our move. The blood on his coat, in the car, *is* Jessica Powell's."
"Well it wouldn't exactly be ketchup, would it?"
Heller took one last puff, before throwing the cigarette on Cowper's shoe. Cowper jumped, clearly outraged.
"But, one thing doesn't add up."
"Oh, and what's that?" Cowper was far too engaged in kicking off the cigarette butt off of his newly polished shoes.
"The description that we had, it had our killer as at least 6'0."
Cowper stopped. "Then, Stevens made a mistake?"
"Hmm. Maybe…"
"Still, surely Green wouldn't have given you a warrant if he knows that."
"Oh, he knows alright. But he wants Hall arrested for something. You see, we arrest him, we search his house and also find those drugs. Not only that, but then Green

has someone arrested in quick time for a murder. Makes his record look good."

"True. I see what you mean, but… I mean he wouldn't risk it would he?"

"It's not the first time…" Heller muttered to himself.

"Huh?"

Heller kept himself to himself, before taking in a large sniff of breath.

"James, I've… I've gotta ask. Do you really think it's Hall?"

The distant detective spun round to face Cowper.

"Why'd you ask?"

Cowper opened his mouth, to which no words came out, at first. "It's just, you hear about all these serial killer cases. Jeffrey Dahmer, take him for example. Took them years to capture him."

"Well, that's because he didn't dump the bodies. He disposed of his first. After doing some fucked up shit to it. But he would have sex with the corpses Greg, cook body parts, keep heads and hands in his fridge. He was clever."

"Then, Jack the Ripper."

"Whoa, my favourite!" Heller chuckled to himself. "See what you mean there. Took ages to capture, well. Nobody. I mean he had five canonical victims, didn't he? But some thought the 6 other Whitechapel Victims were also Ripper victims. Only one could have been though, Martha Tabram, the second Whitechapel Victim. But yeah, the first definite Ripper victim was Mary Ann Nicols. All the Whitechapel Victims after, their injuries were less horrific and blunt to be Jack…" Heller stopped, realising he was sounding like a nerd. Much to Cowper's amusement.

"I just… I just know that the injuries on Powell, those were the signs of a depraved killer, and the letter just about confirms it. A serial killer on the loose. I doubt he'd leave so many clues as to his identity…"

"Sometimes, killers fuck up. Make mistakes. Maybe Hall is the killer, maybe not. But either way, he's implicated, and we'll find the truth."

Heller began to walk back towards the station, before Cowper uttered to him. "There's gonna be another murder."

Heller stopped in his tracks, turning and glaring at the impassive Cowper. With a hesitant nod, Heller made his way back into the station.

Later, in the early evening, Worthing town centre was bustling with activity. Sunday night brought out the partying teens, men and women, attacking the chilling quietness of the town. It wasn't usually quiet, far from it, however the murder of Jessica Powell had left a permanent stain on the town and West Sussex as a whole. But that didn't stop the carefree, almost defiant attitude of everyone. Marching through South Street, as if he owned the town, was the unbeknownst Robert Hall. Emotion-rid face, people would typically keep their distance from the thug. He gave dodgy a bad name. But, he was no gangster by any means, that would be an insult. He wasn't smart, he simply wore Adidas jumpers, Adidas hoodies, Adidas trousers, Adidas everything. Wearing a new, more formal looking coat, thick black,

he made his way towards his regular haunt, the Swallows Return. Passing the Guildbourne Centre, into Warwick Street, Hall noticed that all eyes were on him, judging him. He was far from impressed and grumbled under his breath, right the way till he reached the pub.
Slamming the door open, the jolly and friendly feel of the pub suddenly died down and went mute. Everyone eyed Hall up. It was as though the pub had been drained. Hall rolled up his eyes, and got to the bar past a couple of younger, visibly angry men.
"The usual please Dom." The rusty voice demanded. The silent bartender didn't take his eyes off of Hall, slamming a bottle of Cider in front of Hall. Shamefully, he simply watched Hall. The pub began to slowly regain its usual jovial feel. Jeffrey Stevens also glanced upon Hall as he passed, but halted behind him. Stevens was trying to figure out if he had seen Hall the previous night, even clamping down onto Hall's coat which laid on the seat. Hall hadn't noticed, and Stevens made his getaway with his pint. Blending in, wearing typical clothes for a night out, was Knight. Sitting at a table above a few steps further away from Hall, he took out a small radio.
"He's here. Suspect Robert Hall confirmed to be at the Swallows Return." The robotic voice explained. This was Knight's attempt at being a serious undercover cop.
On the other side of the room, near the entrance, Sergeant John Markham rolled his eyes so far back that he could possibly see his brain.
"Knight, stop putting the radio close to your ear."
He muttered through gritted teeth, his radio concealed in his folded arms. Unlike Knight, Markham was a tall and

imposing man with muscular build, and usually he kept an undefeated expression on his clean-shaven face. "Sorry."
Knight put the radio away in his pocket. He could see, in the corner of his eye, that Hall had taken notice of him. Knight prayed that he hadn't seen the radio. The two undercover officers both kept their eyes distant from Hall. For Knight, the next passing minutes felt like an entire century had gone by. For Markham, he had his eyes set on the prize, an arrest of Robert Hall. Not long after, the doors burst open. Flashing blue lights illuminated Hall's hands. He was far from a stranger to the blues and twos, so immediately turned around to see Heller, Cowper and two PCSOs enter. Hall saw the PCSOs as young, easily handled officers. He regarded Cowper in a similar way, but he knew Heller. Everyone knew who Heller was. But for all the wrong reasons. The good reasons had been wiped from the town's memory. Heller saw Hall the second he entered. The pub had once again been drained, with everyone knowing that the police were there for Hall. Hall, too, knew this. The eyes turned on Hall with hatred, he was the slaughterer of Jessica Powell, and in turn deserved the same fate. At this moment, three men advanced with fury towards Hall.
"Get back!" Heller barked.
Hall then grabbed his bottle and smashed it across the bar, aiming it threateningly at Heller.
"Fuck right off! I didn't even touch that fucking, disgusting slut!" Hall had no cares towards his dead ex, but Heller had no cares towards Hall's attitude, and stepped closer. "I'm warning you! Get back!"

Knight, who had crept close to Hall, grabbed his arm. Hall turned, in surprise. This was when Heller charged at him along with the male PCSO. Hall threw Knight weightlessly to the floor, before punching the PCSO with a loud crack of his nose, joining Knight on a heap on the floor. Heller clamped his arm onto Hall's, struggling with the bottle. Both gritting their teeth, it looked as if it couldn't be broken. Markham and the female PCSO stood close, in case, with Markham armed with handcuffs at the ready. PCSOs could detain but not arrest people, so she felt pretty much helpless. But Superintendent Green wanted nearly all Worthing and local officers at the scene of the murder, which was ridiculous. He saw the PCSOs with very little regard, but they did just as much the same job as any officer.
Anyone in the police shared an equal passion for their job, CSOs or officers, both put their all into their jobs.
Heller, quick thinking, darted his eyes behind Hall. Believing someone was behind him, Hall turned to look, before Heller snapped Hall's arm like a twig, before head battered him then throwing him to the ground by flipping him, pushing him over his foot. Hall came crashing down with an earthquake, to which Markham leapt into action and handcuffed the defeated Hall.
"Robert Hall, I am arresting you on suspicion of the murder of Jessica Powell. You do not have to say anything, but it may harm your defence if you do not mention when questioned something you later rely on in court. Anything you do say may be given in evidence." Heller exclaimed, panting to get his breath back.
Hall was raised up to his feet by Knight, Markham and the two PCSOs.

"I didn't do anything. I had nothing to do with her!" Hall spat.

"Take him to the station." Cowper commanded, with the four other officers escorting an unresisting Hall out of the silent pub.

As Heller grabbed Hall's coat, a knife fell out of the pocket. Landing on the floor, it was covered in dark red blood. Heller and Cowper glanced at each other, before they bagged the bloody knife, with the bartender cleaning away the two droplets of blood. As far as anyone was concerned, Robert Hall was as guilty as sin.

"Come on Cowper." Heller then left the pub very quickly, after downing an unattended drink.

Cowper took one last look around the pub, briefly noticing Stevens, but he focused his sights on someone in particular. In the top corner of the first floor of the pub, watching over the floor, was Mark Hobbes. With dead eyes, Hobbes was simply staring. Unblinking, with six empty glasses piling up on the table. Cowper then quickly left, as Hobbes swayed his arm, before downing his seventh drink.

Chapter Three
Case Closed?

The silent cells of Worthing Station, unusual for a Saturday night, were suddenly filled with the echoing yells from Robert Hall, protesting his innocence. Led by Markham and Knight into the narrow corridor, occupied by cells, they stopped in front of Cell D. Heller tagged along, nodding at the duty officer to unlock the steel cell door.
"Oi! Heller, I'm fucking innocent! You're making a grave mistake mate!" Whined Hall, trying to shake off the officers.
Heller presented the evidence bag, with the knife and a small puddle of blood, in front of an angry Hall.
"Then why was this bloody knife found in your coat pocket? Why was your bloody coat found in the car that *you* stole? That car is filled with fibres of Powell's clothes, and your coat is filled with her blood."
Markham did not approve of Heller's uncontrolled rant.
"Heller, maybe stop telling him before questioning..."
"No Markham, I thought I'd give Hall here a few minutes chance to try and think of an excuse in his cell."
And at that hint, Markham and Knight shoved Hall into the cell, with the duty officer slamming the door shut and locking it. Hall's roaring protests had ceased.

"Shall I take this to forensics for examination, before you burst a blood vessel?" Knight smoothly asked.
Knight's smug attitude would not last long.
"Markham, take this to forensics for examination."
Knight's face dropped as Heller's smiled. Markham nodded as he took the evidence bag, before all three officers left the chillingly silent cells.

Heller was now passing through all the busy corridors, before someone grabbed him. The warm and welcoming Superintendent Charles Green. Green never usually acted like this, often he was a sour faced man who took pride in his sheer authority, doing what he liked, when he liked and looking down his nose upon both police staff and officers.
"Ah, my favourite Detective Inspector!"
"No need to ask why you're so happy sir."
"Well of course! Robert Hall, arrested for murder! I hope your about to interview him?"
"Of course, sir, the mounting evidence against him is, quite frankly, overwhelming."
"Yes, I've seen it. I'm giving you a warrant later to search his premises, find anything else on him."
"Of course you are sir..."
"Ha ha! You know me too well. Listen, the public believe we've got this serial killer before the papers could even attribute one of those cheesy, ominous names to him. So once you've questioned him, I want a statement made by you to the press tomorrow. Faith in Sussex Police, after recent events, shall be restored..." The

fiction filled, posh and pompous sounding voice irritated Heller clearly. He tried to shake it off.
"Sir, I'm afraid I cannot do that. You know full well we cannot confirm in like... Like 12 bloody hours that Hall's the killer, it's unethical and not what we'd usually do. We have 24 hours to question him. I'll tell the media that we have arrested a suspect, but not charged him. Besides, Hall isn't a serial killer if he did indeed kill her. She's the only one."
Green's eye twitched in horror. "No, Heller. That's *not* what I have told you to do. Hall is bingo for us, it's clear he did it!"
Heller got right into Green's face, almost threateningly. "With respect, *sir*, I don't even think he did it."
"What!?"
"A killer wouldn't be this clumsy, if they intended to become a serial killer. Trust me, someone else is going to die."
"Then how'd you explain all the damning evidence? Hmm?"
"I reckon he's been framed."
Green scoffed, before considering. "Very well, make whatever statement you wish. But he will be charged Heller, I'm certain he's the killer! Now get questioning him right away."
Green stormed off, Heller biting his tongue, before hurrying away towards an interview room.

Cowper and Heller sat facing a calmer Hall, having given details of those present in the room, date and time of recording.

"Aren't I allowed to get a lawyer?" Hall grunted.
"We tried to get one for you Hall, but nobody wants to take you on. Not even for the bucket loads of cash, nobody wants to get money because of you and your potential crime." Cowper laid back in his chair.
"I didn't do it!"
Heller shoved a pile of photos in front of Hall.
"These are photos of a VW Tiguan, which you stole two days before the murder. Crime of opportunity, right?"
Hall nodded.
"Well can you explain, in that case, why this car was seen at least half an hour before the murder of Jessica Powell on the A27?"
"Who by?"
"A witness was behind you, in his car. He saw Jessica talking to you, potentially, inside the car."
"Oh come off it! Why the hell would she go anywhere near her ex?"
"This campaign of blackmail, Rob. She's been blackmailing you, about your stash of drugs, hasn't she?"
Hall nodded at Cowper.
"I take it that's my motive, is it?"
"You tell us."
Silence.
"No."
Heller drew forward.
"Then you're saying you had a motive, but not this one?"
"No! Your twisting my words! I had no motive because I haven't killed her, how many more times?" Hall pleaded.
"Where were you between the hours of 11:00PM on Friday 21st and 1:00AM on Saturday 22nd September Rob?"

Hall sighed.

"I... I was at home, with that stash. Trying to get rid of it so Jessica could stop blackmailing me. And no, I don't have an alibi."

Heller and Cowper glanced at each other, raising their eyebrows.

"Can you explain why we have Jessica's blood in your coat and in the car?" Cowper turned back.

"No! But I reckon someone like... Like must have framed me. Or she just killed herself to make it look like I did it."

"And she managed to practically perform a living autopsy on herself?"

"Well Heller, you know all too well about faked murders, turning out to be suicides."

Heller sharply darted his eyes at the smug Hall who was nodding to himself.

"Alright, let's just get it all clear for the purposes of the recording. You stole a car, the VW Tiguan, from a petrol station near the beach. Two days later, you use it to meet up with Jessica for some kind of arrangement, where you take her to Clapham Woods and put an end to her twisted little games of blackmail, correct?"

Hall had desperately been shaking his head.

"No, no... It's not true!"

"Then explain all the evidence against you!" Cowper shouted.

Hall was left silent.

In the office, Heller ushered Cowper to his office. Once in, Heller punched the door shut.

"Maybe I was wrong, maybe he *is* the killer." Heller suggested.
Cowper agreed.
"Well so far, it certainly looks like it. He had no alibi. Look James, he said to us before the interview ended that he had smoked up his entire stash. You're getting a warrant, right? So if we find the stash there then we'll know that he's lying to us."
Heller nodded, before hurrying over to his desk and taking a bottle of whiskey from the drawer, which he began to take violent swigs from.
"Whoa, sir!"
Heller held out his hand, commandingly, stopping Cowper in his tracks after having a few more gulps.
"He brought up Raph Thomas."
"Who?"
"Raph Thomas." Heller threw the bottle away and slammed the drawer shut. "Case I worked on, suicide big time. But it affected so many people, the suspects, friends, family... Even us, the police. The fucking nerve! He cut his ex up like a dog chewing ragged meat!"
"Alright, alright. Try and calm down. Maybe get rid of that bottle?"
"Nah, I keep it with me whenever I wanna celebrate a solved case, this was just a one off. But goes no further than this room, okay Greg?"
"You trust me to not snitch on you?" Cowper smiled.
"Well, you're not quite Ralph Knight, are you?" Both men chuckled.
"You know, I'm not just here as another DI. I'm here as your friend."

Heller glanced up at Cowper. Heller was smiling, clearly touched by the gesture. It had been a long time since anyone took an interest in his problems, it was something he's got used to by now. He sniffed, nodding.
"Thanks man. You too you know, I mean I'll... I'll be here as your friend too."
Heller was awkward at getting his words out, but Cowper knew he meant well. Then, the door swung open, as Green entered, holding with him a search warrant.
"Inspector, the search warrant for Robert Hall's property, given by the magistrates. I told them there would be drugs there after his questioning. About the drugs."
"Thanks sir." Heller took the warrant, turning to Cowper. "Under section 8 of the Police and Criminal Evident Act, I Guess we'll see if he's telling the truth."

That Sunday morning, Hall was not prepared for the blaring voice of Heller to be blurting like a klaxon in his ears.
"Once again Robert, what were you doing on the night that Jessica was murdered!?"
"I told you! You need to open your ears mate!" Hall began to get angry too.
Heller nodded mockingly before opening a folder, revealing photos of cannabis plants, several messy trails of cocaine on a dirty grubby table and three needles on a burnt carpet floor.
"Then what's all that Rob? Cocaine ready, but unused. Cannabis plants, for your dealing. Needles, again, ready but unused."
Hall was silent.

"Again Rob, this is one of the most important questions that I need to ask you. Let's say you are innocent, okay. If so, who used the car that you stole? And how, if you had the keys?"

Hall inhaled, and gulped.

"Well, I mean it weren't my car, so I didn't care too much about it. I could easily steal another. But the night of her murder, I was at the Traveller's Inn. I remember, I was drunk. But I just left the keys on the bar, for anyone to take for a spin if they have me a couple of quid. Just for jokes. I didn't get it back."

Heller and Cowper sighed, at the same time, in frustration.

"What?" Hall was confused.

"I really wish we could believe that Rob, but we already asked everyone in that pub after we arrested you, if you were at the pub that night. All who were there that night, said you weren't." Cowper admitted.

"Then they're lying! They just think I did it because of my... My mistakes, with Jessica."

"Look, there is CCTV of the car passing through South Street, across the seafront then round that alleyway, at around..." Heller checked several papers. "Ten that evening. But the person who gets out of the car, is wearing a plain black hoodie, with the hood up."

Heller pressed photos of the black hooded figure in the CCTV, getting out of the car.

"Is that you, Rob?"

Hall shook his head.

"I'm gonna tell the truth, I can't remember. I was absolutely plastered that night!"

Heller took another, focused, look at the CCTV images. He sighed.

"You know I really wanna believe that you did to drive the car, to pick her up. Then brutally murder her and mutilate her. But you're not giving us any evidence that you were elsewhere."

"Surely the pub has CCTV?"

Cowper shook his head. "They don't."

"You see, you have a fair amount of stubble Robert. The killer was seen to have stubble, underneath all that stubble."

"All that I can tell you is that I had *nothing* to do with it! Nothing at all!" Hall then collapsed into his arms.

"The only evidence supporting that you possibly aren't the killer is very minimal. There aren't any photos of Jessica's body at your home." Cowper then put the photos back into the folder.

"Well there wouldn't be, cause I didn't do it…"

"Do you own a polaroid camera?" Cowper asked.

"If you do, maybe you destroyed it…" Heller remarked, waiting to see the responses from Hall.

"No!"

"You have enough money to get another one, they're like… One hundred odd quid, I have one, I know."

"Maybe you did it then." Hall smirked.

"I think you *did* do it, Hall. To stop the blackmail, you met up with her and you sadistically humiliated her, ripping her open. You didn't have enough time to cover your tracks, so you write us a letter and print it out in advance, leaving it in Clapham Woods, to throw us off of the scent that you targeted her, making it look like it was a random serial killer!"

"No!" Hall rose up, to which Heller got up too, ushering him with his hand to sit down. Hall obediently did so. "Interview terminated at... 5:30PM, Sunday 23rd September." Heller announced, as he grabbed Cowper's arm and took him out of the interview room.

In the corridor, Heller and Cowper were standing by the water cooler. Cowper swallowed the entire contents of his cup in under ten seconds, before tossing it into a bin.
"I reckon we have no serial killer on our hands, and he's just made that up."
"I have to disagree, but given the evidence, we've gotta charge him." Heller moaned.
"Well, Green's gonna be pleased."
"I'm not, an innocent man held on remand for murder. That's the way I see it. This killer has framed him, but we cannot prove this."
"But... But if your right, surely there's a way in which we can prove what you say?"
"There isn't. We're just gonna have to wait till murder number 2."
The words chilled Cowper, as Heller slowly walked away. Cowper was beginning to reconsider his thoughts, but the confusion of his first murder case was not going to get too much for him. He was determined.

That Monday morning, it was highly overcast across the town of Worthing. Gathered for the latest news outside the station, was the media. They were like a violent mob, trying to get closer to Heller who was standing with all

cameras and microphones pinioned on him, the flashes making his eyes ache and ache even more. He felt extremely lethargic, but cleared his throat. Standing with him were two officers and Cowper.
"Good morning, thank you, thank you." The crowd began to calm down. "I can confirm, that 45-year-old Robert Hall, has been formally charged for the murder of Jessica Powell, who was murdered in Clapham Woods on Friday 21st September, just before midnight of Saturday 22nd…"
As Heller continued on in his monotone voice, watching from the back of the crowds, was a greying old man. He wore a parka jacket, hands stuffed into the pockets and wearing a flat peak cap, which he used to keep his vision low down. He had a disturbed, yet disturbing, looking face. Rotten yellow teeth, that remained, bit his dry lips. This, was Nathan Emerson. Emerson had good reason, so he would presume, to keep his head down. An ex-rapist, who horrifically raped 4 young girls in the area of Worthing in the 80s, who had been released from prison. It was known that he'd been released, but very few other than the police knew that he had returned. Heller briefly caught sight of the old man, who also shared a glance. Heller knew who he was immediately. Nobody could forget the haunting face of that man in the papers, back in 87. Emerson smiled, twistedly, before heading off in the direction of Chapel Road, waving bye to Heller as he went on his way. As he passed the Slug and Lettuce Pub, covered in scaffolding, the almost proud Emerson, found his hat was hit to the ground. Alarmed, he bolted round very quickly for someone in their mid-70s, to see four hooded men, circling around him. Before he could utter a

word in his foul breath, the men pounced on him. Much to the horror of younger people running away, the older people in the street recognised him immediately. Within seconds, Emerson was dribbling blood from his mouth, blood trickling down from both nostrils, and his face was already a dark purple from the beatings. The men said nothing, but threw the paedophile to the ground, before jumping on him. Passing where Emerson had, Knight and Markham turned to see one of the men stamp on Emerson's face.

"Oi!" Markham yelled in his gruff voice.

The men then instantly took off, looking through their balaclavas to see the two officers.

"Knight, stay with him and get an ambulance. I'll give chase! All available units, four men have just assaulted an elderly gentleman, heading down Chapel Road towards South Street…!" Markham sped off.

Knight knelt beside Emerson, who spat out one of his rotten teeth, before grunting and scoffing.

He smiled and simply whispered. "I'm back!" before passing out.

Heller was in his office, reading the report of the assault on Emerson. Only two of the men had been arrested, and were smiling joyfully in their mugshot photos.

"And he said, 'I'm back…' before passing out." Knight was being like an OTT theatre actor.

"Yeah, thanks for that Knight." Heller threw the papers onto his desk as he drunk his coffee.

"But.. Sir, don't you feel that it's relevant?"

"To what exactly?"

Knight's mouth dropped. "Well, maybe, just... Maybe, the murder case you've been put on."
Heller shook his head. "Nope."
"But he said that he's back, with that... Ugly, rank smile... He might mean that he's back, but this time to murder!"
"Nope."
Knight was not done yet. "Then he possibly raped Powell!"
"Nope. You know full well that there were no signs of any sexual activity in the autopsy. Anyway, leave it for whoever is handling it. But, we'll keep note of Emerson. He's a sexual deviant, we all know that. It's worth keeping note."
"Well, I thought it would be worth telling you."
"Thanks Ralph, though I had already thought of it. If another body turns up, then we'll have to take a look at any sex offender within... 10 miles."
Ralph nodded and then turned to leave, before pausing. "Erm, sir. Rob Hall was charged. You even did it, don't you remember?"
Heller got up and checked through piles and piles of paperwork. "Of course I do. He's been charged because of the evidence against him, but I know murder, Knight. I know it very well. But then there's serial murders, and I know those quite well too. Jessica was the victim of a serial killer, and I highly doubt it was Hall."
"Jesus... Well, you'd better tell Green."
"Yeah, like that'd do any good." Heller chuckled.
"Then what are we meant to do!? Wait till someone else gets killed?"

"Unfortunately, yes. Green won't allow for extra officers out in the streets, because he thinks we've already got the man. I asked him, trust me."

Knight nodded, clearly annoyed about this. As he turned to leave, Cowper rushed in with another man. This man, who wore a shirt and 70's style sweater over it, was short and had large glasses on the edge of his nose.

"Oh, great. The renowned Eddie Stubbs of the Worthing Herald. So, what displeasure do I owe you?"

"*Edward* Stubbs, actually Inspector." Stubbs corrected in a vexed tone.

Heller nodded.

"Well, yes. Edward Stubbs is a displeasure in himself, I quite agree."

Ralph tried to hide his smile by glancing down at the floor.

"Sir, Mr. Stubbs here received a letter. I think you'll wanna take a look at this."

Heller was about to make another joke, but saw the serious tempered face of Cowper. Heller's tone dropped. "Right, let's have a look.

"We found it in the post, in an unmarked envelope, as you can see." Stubbs opened the envelope, continuing on in his nerdy, high pitched and almost whiny voice. "It's from the killer, Inspector."

Heller stopped, glancing up at Stubbs. Stubbs was serious too. Heller then opened the already torn envelope and took out the letter. It was folded finely, and like the letter found in Clapham Woods, was printed out. It read:

"**To the Worthing Herald,**

Ah, how the police try and try to convince you all that they have their killer. I can tell you that they have the wrong man, hand to heart. Literally, as you shall soon see. I find it rather amusing, to watch these puny little insects work and work away, using Robert Hall as a scapegoat. I know how DI James Heller's mind works, and he knows full well that they have the wrong man. Can't argue against orders from the high ups, is my guess.
But you'll see the truth, very soon. I shall say in advance, may the next victim rest in pieces.

Kind regards,
The Midnight Murderer"

Heller's hands were shaking. Not in fear, but in anger.

Later, the office was entirely clear of Knight and Stubbs, with only Cowper, Green and Heller himself there.
"I'm telling you sir, this is *not* a hoax!" Heller had a note of desperation in his voice.

"Detective Inspector! If this was real, it would be sent to *us*!"
"No sir, us and the press. Don't you see? He's trying to scare the public, make us look weak and unprofessional!"
"It's fake, end of!" Green spun away and opened the door.
"Hall is innocent." Heller remarked.
Green, gritting his teeth, shook his head in despair and slammed the door shut. Heller turned to Cowper.
"Fucking twat! What a cunt!" he smashed the letter onto the table. "Any other superintendent would take an interest! But him, no! Oh no, he's *got* to be right!"
"Okay, calm down mate…"
"No, Greg. I can't! He's… He's…"
Cowper tried to latch onto what Heller was saying.
"What? He's what?"
"Corrupt." Heller whispered.
"Corrupt? Oh, come on James. A right wanker, maybe, but corrupt?"
"Trust me, I know he is. I know more than anyone else."
"But why should I believe you man? And I mean, how do you know?"
Heller turned to open the draw, but stopped himself. He took his eyes onto Cowper.
"Well, you trust me, right?"
Cowper nodded quickly.
"Then that's the answer to your first question. Second, well… If you're gonna be corrupt, you're not gonna be successful if everyone knows about it, are you?"
Heller then stormed out of the room, grabbing his lighter from the desk as he left.

Cowper remained, in stunned silence. He then took a look at the desk, before walking round to it, sitting down in the warm seat. The desk was littered in an explosion of papers, but two photo frames caught Cowper's eye. The first, near the angle poise lamp, was of Heller. He looked younger, with maintained stubble and hair, but was smiling. Not smiling like he did now, whenever he joked, but genuine happiness. He was standing with quite an attractive woman, both dressed up. Then, the other frame was next to it. Heller looked the exact same as in the other photo, also smiling. With him, was Markham. But next to Markham, was a man who Cowper didn't recognise. He wore a suit, and must have been part of CID like Heller. He had silver, spiked and rather fine hair. Shorter than both men, they looked like the best of buds. Cowper then glanced at the drawers. Curiously, he drew the first open. Removing the nearly empty bottle of whisky, was a folder. On it, were the words:

```
      "Raph Thomas
     Murder Case #4
        10.1.2012
          SOLVED"
```

Attached with a paperclip, were several photos. Cowper took them off and scanned through them. The first was of a dead body, skyscraper high grass surrounding it. It was a young man, with a bloody gunshot wound to the head. There were several of him, then others of him on the autopsy table. After, were five mugshots of different men. Then, there was a photo of another dead man, in a car park it seemed. This man, however, was the same man in the photo frame. He looked as if he'd been stabbed, in the other photos too. Cowper was deep in thought, but put them back in the drawer with the whiskey bottle. One thing was for certain though, Heller was hiding something, and it sure as hell was eating away at him.

Thursday, October 4th. The streets of the town centre were rid of pretty much anyone. Distant cars passing by on the rain flooded roads of the previous night were heard now and then, barking dogs here and there. In Field Row, a long and very narrow stretch of road in Worthing, was never the welcoming home to sounds at night. The first part was on the edge of Montague Street, and was filled with the backs of shops and stores, but also the home to small shops towards the end. Then, a gap where Shelly Road was, but all that separated the row was a road, before the rest of Field Row resembled an abandoned, litter filled alleyway. It may as well have been an alleyway, with a few houses. It then led off to Ambrose Place, which was a spacious and much more inviting site, with some of the most expensive houses in the town centre. A resident of Field Row, much to her anger, was to be woken up by the sound of running across the cobbles, getting further away towards Ambrose Place. Claire, the resident, grabbed her dressing gown and tied it tight, before throwing the door open. The outside felt like Antarctica. The wind was even howling, but the echoing and nearby sound of the Town

Hall clock chiming on midnight was bellowing across the town. Folding her arms to try and keep herself warm, Claire looked up towards the end of the row. She saw nobody. Then, she glanced down. Something had caught her eye, a pair of legs, with bloodstained jeans. The stains were minimal and dark, but when Claire shone her phone torch onto them, they were fresh and hadn't even soaked in yet. Gulping, Claire prudently got closer and closer, where next to an old tin dustbin, laid a horrifically mutilated corpse. It resembled a paint brush being flung on paper. Gasping in horror, she dropped her phone and stood back towards the wall, before she felt a squelch. Gagging, she saw on the ground, a fresh red heart lying in a small puddle of blood.

Chapter Four
Heartless

It was only gone 12:05AM, and Field Row was littered with police activity. Heller glanced miserably at the body. The young woman had been subjected to sheer horrors. Her eyes were stabbed repeatedly, her mouth open and gushing with blood, for her tongue ad been sliced off and was nowhere to be seen. Her breasts had been sliced off, tossed into the bin she was laying against. Her throat had been slit right back to the spine, with her stomach literally ripped open. Her intestines and kidneys had been removed and placed behind her, one on top of the other. Her jeans were completely red in blood, where her genitals were. This was a frenzied, horrific attack. Heller then felt the blinding flash of a camera to his left. He turned to see Stubbs photographing the body. "Get him the fuck away from here! Now!" Heller snapped.
Two officers then spoke briefly to Stubbs as he was escorted away from the police ribbon, waving in the breeze. Cowper was standing with a neighbour, who kept rattling on without taking time to breathe.
"Just before midnight, 11:58PM, I saw on my alarm clock. I peered through the curtains, because I heard something fall against a bin. I saw someone, running. Wearing a black hoodie, black dickies. I saw the Dickies

logo as I looked at them running further up the alleyway."

Cowper nodded, finishing writing notes.

"Right, thank you Mr. Hopper. I must ask, did this man have a backpack on him?"

"Not as far as I'm aware, no."

"Excuse me one moment sir." Cowper then wandered over to Heller.

"I knew we got it wrong, I knew it. And it cost her life." Heller sighed. "Such a waste..."

"Heller, just got a witness statement. A neighbour saw the killer run up towards Ambrose Place, *without* a backpack."

"Hmm... We need to have the victim identified as quickly as possible, then we can get a clearer picture of her final hours. As for Hall, he'll be cleared of Jessica's murder, but remain on demand for the drugs."

"Inspector!" A cry from Markham came from Ambrose Place.

Both detectives glanced at each other, frowning.

"You or me?" Heller asked, before they both headed up towards the end if the alleyway.

They reached four officers, being guided by Markham. They had opened a drain, which was flowing with lots of murky, filthy water. Floating, was a black backpack. Heller inhaled through gritted teeth as it was placed on the ground. With his clean white gloves, Heller zipped the bag open.

"Let's hope nothing inside is damaged." Cowper said as he knelt beside Heller. Heller opened the bag and took out a Polaroid camera.

"Letter! Look for a letter!"

"Yes sir." Markham indicated the officers to help him search the alleyway for a letter.
Heller took a good look at the Polaroid, a large bulky thing.
"That's the exact one I have! Vintage... 600, something like that. It's a remake of the old ones, got it from Urban Outfitters." Cowper declared.
Heller nodded.
"You know whose camera this belongs to Gregory my friend?"
"Who?"
Heller showed Cowper the bottom of the camera, with a damp label with a name on.
"Mark Hobbes."
Both Cowper and Heller raised their eyebrows, curiously.

In the lonely and cold, light blue tinted mortuary at Worthing Hospital, Heller and Cowper stood above the body of the young woman. Dr. Cuthbertson was washing his hands in the sink. A respected man, with a deep bellowing and posh voice, he was no stranger to horrifying injuries.
"Yes, shoved in between her small intestines, which as I've explained were stabbed and severed. From the stab wounds on her legs, I'd say the blade was 7 inches at least."
Heller rolled his eyes.
"Yes, right. But the letter. The one found in her intestines doctor."
"Hmm? Oh, yes! Over here."

Cuthbertson threw the water off his hands onto Cowper, without realising. He then brought the two detectives over to an ice-cold metal table, where a bloody envelope was in an evidence bag. It had been folded several times.

"Stuffing it in her body... That's fucking grim." Cowper blurted.
"He's just showing off. If you want my advice, your killer doesn't know much about the body. He hasn't carefully found each body part that's been removed, he's just guessed and mounted a frenzied attack. But he's got to be strong to slice the body open in the way that he did. It looks as if he strangled her, due to the amount of bruising in her neck, to subdue her. This also reduces the amount of blood splatter, so I doubt your killer would have blood stains on his clothes." Cuthbertson concluded.
Before Heller or Cowper could say a word, Cuthbertson had walked out. The room was left in silence, except from the monotonous muttering of the cold chambers. Heller and Cowper moved closer to each other.
"This time, he wasn't interrupted. He had a long time, and I agree with Cuthbertson. He has very little medical knowledge, it was all random." Heller explained, deep in thought.
He then out his glasses on and opened the evidence bag.

"Shouldn't we open it at the station?"
"Nah." Heller decided as he opened the envelope, covered in blood.
The letter opened, with blood on it. But the font could be seen. A Polaroid of the victim slipped out, then another.

One was a close up of her face, the other a shot of her body lying against the bin, showing the full extent of her injuries. Heller began to read the letter out aloud, which read:

```
"Dear Detective Inspector Heller,


You are smart, and you knew this would
happen. I had a gut feeling you'd
think that...
You won't stand a chance of catching
me, not while I'm only just starting.
I'm having fun. So, I'll help you with
a clue. I'm much closer to home than
you'd think, Inspector. Watching the
police think they're on the right
track really does give me the shits! I
was gonna take a selfie with her, but,
that'd be insulting for you to have me
leave my identity on a platter for
you.


Good luck,
The Midnight Murderer"
```

Heller gritted his teeth, the letter taunting him.
"He's smug ain't he?" Heller put all the evidence back in the bag before walking away in thoughtfulness.

Outside the Hospital, which wasn't too busy at 1:30AM in the dark, bitter morning, Heller took a swig from another whiskey bottle, before admiring the burning taste. Cowper then came around the corner.
"Got the autopsy report from Cuthbertson-" Cowper broke off as Heller stuffed the bottle back in his coat.
"James!" He was now very stern.
"It was just a one off..."
"Yeah, just like the other time." Cowper bitterly fumed as he took the bottle and threw it into a bin. "Look, I dunno what happened before. All I know is that you took like, like a year off. But what's eating away at you, so much, that you drink? On the job!"
Heller said nothing.
"You've gotta stop man, I don't wanna lose this case! Do you?"
"Of course not..."
"Well then, stop drinking away your problems! You can't rely on alcohol to wipe away your problems. Especially Jack Daniels."
Heller laughed to himself, before smiling at Cowper.
"Your right. The drinking stops, today! We've got work to do!"
Heller enthusiastically got into the patrol car, with Cowper, as they sped off out of the quiet hospital car park.

Later that morning, just after daybreak, a resentful Green growled as he saw Hall leave the station from Heller's office on the first floor. Hall, carrying a small bag full of his clothes, bar the two coats, clenched his fists. He turned to see Green, giving him an utterly hateful look, before storming away.

"How could we possibly have got it wrong!? All the evidence against him" Green turned away from the window in disgust and defeat.

Heller spun round, smiling, in his chair. "Easily explained sir. Hall was framed. Yes, he stole the car. But I believe him. That Friday night, he was pretty much paralytic, so someone stole the keys to use the car, which had his coat inside. So the killer may have been in the pub when we arrested him. But how the bloody knife was planted on him, and when, I dunno."

"Hmm. Did you get the results of the knife?"

"Yes, it was Jessica Powell's blood."

"Well, Hall's been released on bail for the drugs and car theft. He'll be back here soon enough." Green chuckled.

"Heller." Cowper rushed in, slamming a newspaper onto the desk in front of Heller. The cover photo was of Heller, noticing Stubbs who took the photo, with the body next to him. It had been heavily censored. But, on the upper right corner, a photo of a young, blonde and smiling woman was seen.

Heller read, without his glasses. "Abby Luther, 23… Confirmed victim…"

"Yeah, we've just identified her fingertips. She was arrested last year for drunk and disorderly conduct." Cowper then showed Heller a drunken mugshot photo of Luther.

"Well you guys, I have something quite interesting for you. A lot of interesting things actually."

Cowper and Green sat around Heller. Heller put in a videotape into a small, bulky TV on the desk. He fast forwarded slightly grainy CCTV to the timestamp. It shows, in slow frame by frame, a black hooded figure, quite tall, walking with a smaller woman. The woman had blonde hair, and was Luther. The pair walked into Field Row at this time. Heller then fast forwarded to 12:06AM, to which the other side of Field Row was seen by Ambrose Place. In similar quality, the killer runs, but stops as he dumps the backpack into a drain, before running further up Ambrose Place out of view.

"That's our killer, and he's deliberately dumped the bag. Not dropped it, *dumped*. Also..." Heller took out his notepad. "A couple spoke to me at the cordon after we went back there, after the mortuary. They said, at around 10:45PM, they saw the deceased with a man on the seafront, opposite the Dome Cinema. They are certain it's her. This man had a yellow jumper, a winter coat, black backpack and a black cap. He saw them and bolted his head down, using the cap to try and hide his face presumably."

"So he got changed again..." Cowper realised. "But then, where's the yellow jumper and winter coat?"

"We must presume that he kept the yellow jumper on. He must have put his hoodie on over it just after 11:30PM, as he was seen with Luther on CCTV in South Street with the hoodie. But the coat and hat... I dunno where they are. Officers are searching for them."

"He got rid of them somewhere before killing her." Green suggested.

"Erm… Yes, thanks sir. Great help." Was the sarcastic response from Heller. "Anyway, we need to speak to Mark Hobbes. Why was his camera there? In the bag."

Hobbes was sitting in his home, a one floor flat, made in houses. The window overlooked Victoria Park, on a crisp morning. He was trying to watch TV, but he was always distracted by the disturbing thought of the killer watching him constantly, pulling all the strings. He then glanced at a broken window, in the living room, which was covered on the other side with a small wooden board. Then, a thundering knock at the door made Hobbes jump out of his skin. He slowly got up and went into the hallway where the other flats were. Hobbes breathed in, and quickly opened the door, to see Heller and Cowper, with Knight behind them. Both men showed their badges.
"Mark Hobbes, I'm DI James Heller, you've previously spoken to my colleague, DI Greg Cowper."
Hobbes was totally relieved. "Oh, yes. Yes. Can I help you?"
"Well, may we come in?"

Soon, Heller and Cowper were sitting in the living room. Hobbes entered with a tray full of two coffees, his hands shaking. Knight stood near the door.
"Two coffees." Hobbes placed the tray on a table.
"Thank you." Heller walked across to the window.
"What happened to your window?"
"Dunno, someone threw a rock through the window like, on the 2nd. I was out photographing a wedding couple."

"You a photographer then Mark?" Cowper sipped his coffee.

"Yes, the only way I get more money than a dead-end job with the minimum wage."

"Why didn't you report this to the police?" Heller was taking a good look at the smash.

"Well, you were dealing with one murder then. Didn't see it as a pressing matter."

Heller looked around the room. "Was anything stolen? This entire part of the window was smashed, enough room for someone to break in."

"Well, nothing was taken as far as I'm aware of. Probably just some kids."

Heller then presented to Hobbes an evidence bag, containing the polaroid camera found in the backpack. "Is this yours, Mark?"

Mark had a good look. "Yes. Yes, I think so. I mean it should have my name on the bottom."

Heller showed Hobbes the bottom of the camera, with the sticker. "Mark, this was found in a backpack in a drain where Abby Luther was murdered."

Hobbes' gulped, but interestingly did appear too alarmed. "I... I can't explain that sir. It could have been stolen. I never use it anymore, kept it in my study."

"May we check your study?" Cowper got up.

"Yes, this way officers..." Hobbes led the two detectives and Knight to his room, which had a single bed and shelves full of different cameras and tripods. He had, simply, a laptop on his bed which was off. Hobbes noticed that in a cabinet of older, vintage cameras, the place where his polaroid once was, had gone. His mouth dropped.

"My… God! I hadn't even realised… but it *has* been stolen!"

"How on earth do you not realise a large polaroid camera like that has been taken from your cabinet? There's even dust surrounding the whole cabinet, except from the shape of where the polaroid was." Heller took out his notebook.

"I'm sorry, I just didn't!"

Heller was already scribbling down. "Where were you between the hours of 10:00PM yesterday evening and 12:30AM this morning?"

All eyes were on Hobbes. He was stuttering. "H… Here. Alone. But I can't back this up. But I did go to the nearby shop at around 11:00, the door's loud, you could ask my neighbours."

"Knight will attend to that, although even if they did, it could be anyone." Heller nodded at Knight as he left the room. "What store did you go to?"

"Tesco Express. It's near Worthing Station."

Cowper, who was also writing, stopped. "I know that Tesco. I worked there when I was 18, waiting for my application to join the force. That Tesco Express closes at 10:00PM."

Heller inhaled as Hobbes began to clearly sweat. "Why are you lying to us Mr. Hobbes?"

Knight was about to open the door in the living room, which led to the compact hallway. He stopped, seeing a bin bag beside the sofa. Curiously, he opened it. Mouth opening wide, Knight took out a black baseball cap, followed by the same winter coat that the killer wore.

"Sir!" He cried out. It wasn't long before Heller, Cowper and Hobbes joined Knight.

"Hmm, good find Knight." Heller knelt down to take a closer look. "Mark, this is rather interesting. You know why?"

"N… No."

Heller turned. "These are exactly what the killer wore last night, before he got changed."

"Well, I'm sure it's just coincidence."

"They weren't found anywhere near the scene. In fact, they weren't found at all. Until now." Cowper added.

"They aren't mine, I swear!"

Heller got right up. "Whose are they then?"

Hobbes was silent.

"We're gonna need to take these as evidence. As you say, it could be coincidence."

"James…!" Cowper was shocked.

"Quiet a minute." Heller turned back to Hobbes. "We may need you at the station at some point for questioning."

Hobbes nodded. "Right."

Heller and Cowper then walked off back into the bedroom, talking in hushed whispers.

"James, why aren't you arresting him!? Those are what the killer wore!"

"Don't you think, by the look of him, we should leave it? Have him watched, constantly, to see what he does? Of course we will analyse the clothes, but trust me, it's better this way."

Heller hurried away as Cowper sighed in frustration.

Back in Heller's office, Cowper, Knight and Markham were waiting. The sounds of officers in the common room, shuffling out in conversation, were heard. Heller then opened the door, and closed it right behind him.
"Sorry for waiting guys."
"Look, what's all this about Heller? Hear you didn't arrest Mark Hobbes!"
"Well, Markham. We don't need to arrest him. We need to keep an eye on him."
Markham frowned for an answer.
"The coat and hat are currently being analysed, but Hobbes isn't the killer. Knight, explain."
Knight moved forward. "Yes. Hobbes didn't go to the Tesco Express near the train station, but at 10:50PM, he went round by the bike shelter at the station. There, he left the coat and hat. At 11:00PM, the killer picked them up and headed to the town centre."
There was a stunned silence.
"This means that the couple who saw the killer and Luther on the seafront got the time wrong, but their phones were out of battery. Easy mistake. But we must assume that Hobbes is working with the killer. Now, if we arrest him, the killer loses an ally. So there'll be less for us to work on. Do you seriously expect Hobbes to give us much answers? I know people like him, and they won't."
Heller put his arms round Knight and Markham's shoulders.
"You two, I'm gonna need you to carry out a surveillance op on Mr. Hobbes, starting from tonight."
Knight smiled enthusiastically, while Markham rolled his eyes, once again.

In some council flats, somewhere on the edge of Worthing, Heller and Cowper were walking across the landing of the sixth floor. Cowper was being dragged like a slow dog.
"Why are *we* taking a look? This isn't our department."
"Nathan Emerson, we all know who he is. You and I both know he got beat up, rightfully so…"
"And?"
"Well, I've just kept his name down in the case. This is just to have a little insight into him."
"Heller, it wasn't him."
"Okay, so who is the killer then?"
Cowper was speechless. They reached No.46, to which Heller hammered on the door. After a brief wait, Emerson creaked open the door. His face resembled that of a cauliflower ear.
"Yes, yes… I called the police." His twisted, almost childlike voice popped out.
"Yes Mr. Emerson, that's why we're here. May we come in?" Heller asked.

Heller and Cowper were in the cramped, tiny flat. It consisted of one room, stinking of alcohol and smoke. Emerson fell back in his tatty old chair.
"You're the detective on the murders, aren't you? Both of you, the Midnight Murders."
"That's right sir, we are." Cowper then got out his notepad as Heller marched around the flat, being watched bitterly by Emerson. "So, your being harassed you say?"

"Yes, yes. Particularly by the general public, as you know, four of those fucking thugs beat the fucking shit out of me the other day! *You* lot only caught two of them!"

"Well better than none, and we could easily have let them escape without chasing them. You must understand why they did what they did?"

Emerson blinked, a lot. "Something that is well in the past…"

"Four fucking rapes! Pedo you are." Heller cried out. "Dirty fucking pig."

"James, calm down. Please." Cowper was trying to control the situation. "Go on Mr. Emerson."

"Well, they come here, hammering on the door. This is a council estate, isn't it? I can't even go outside anymore. They all go for me. And it doesn't help that the country, even the world press, is here in Sussex anyway because of those murders, but they also pester me. That Eddie Skelt even published an article, saying that *I* could be the killer!"

"And are you?"

Emerson hesitated, perhaps for shock or something else. "No."

Cowper watched him, before noting the rest down.

Elsewhere, in his trapped world, Hobbes was sitting at the table in his living room, head in his hands. His phone sat on the table, where a text could be seen.

"Mark, good morning.

As I pull the strings, you will shave the stubble that you have, and cut a clump of hair off your head. With this clump of hair, you'll put it in an envelope and leave it in the bin near Costa at the Bandstand. If not, I shall use another camera of yours that I stole in the next murder. You don't want to be caught in the act, do you?

Thank you,
The Midnight Murderer"

Hobbes shakily sighed. When he read the end of the text, he frowned in confusion. He then bolted up and headed straight for his room. He checked the shelves and cabinet, but no cameras were seemingly missing. "The disposables…" he then looked under his bed, almost like he was preparing himself to see a monster under the bed. There was a box, full of three disposable cameras. Hobbes reluctantly pulled the box out, and to his horror, the fourth disposable camera was missing. The killer had complete control of Hobbes.

In the common room, several officers had once again gathered the next morning.
"Right, good morning." Cowper yawned. "DI Heller is arranging a surveillance op on Mark Hobbes, so I'll be going over this for you. Now then, Robert Hall as we know has been released, but as usual with a case such as this, we must keep him on the radar, however he was very likely framed. Mark Hobbes, is now a priority. We all know why he's a suspect, we spoke over it, but like I

said we are going to have a surveillance op on him. Nathan Emerson."

Everyone hissed and chattered away.

"Highly unlikely, as neither Jessica Powell nor Abby Luther were sexually assaulted, but due to his background, we must bare him in mind. Make some door to door enquiries at Emerson's council estate, see whether neighbours know where he was on the dates of the murders. We can't ask him as if he doesn't get onto us, the more likely he is to take the bait and do something next time, if he is involved. Okay, that's all guys."

All the officers then got back to chattering as they left the common room. Cowper looked thoughtfully at the map of Worthing and the surrounding areas of where both women were murdered, along with the mugshots and details of Mark Hobbes, Robert Hall and Nathan Emerson. He took a deep breath in.

In his office, Heller had finished his monologue to Knight and Markham about the operation to watch Hobbes. Markham looked far less enthusiastic than Knight, who was beaming.

"Right, that's it then. Get ready you two."

"Yes sir." They both said, far differently to each other, however, before leaving the office and passing Cowper. Cowper closed the door behind him.

"They're gonna be heading to Hobbes' address, we have a total of two weeks, Green mustn't find out, and the team aren't willing to tell him anytime soon."

"So, out of the three suspects, who do you think it is?"

Heller stopped drinking his coffee, frozen. He then put it onto the table. "You mean two? Hall isn't a suspect, we're just keeping an eye on him. But, out of Hobbes and Emerson, you know I'm gonna say Hobbes. All the things we found at his house, in the backpack. What about you?"
Cowper pondered for a few moments. "None of them. I think Emerson has nothing to do with them, he's a rapist, not a killer. But, can't rule out the idea that he's swayed to murdering now instead. Hobbes, like Hall, wouldn't make himself look this guilty. Somethings going on, but either way, he has some involvement in the situation."
Heller nodded, deep in thought.

Hobbes was out in the fresh air, something he hadn't done for a while. He strolled, head down, like a child in a strop. He was in Liverpool Gardens, which overlooked the Bandstand in the town centre. Driving slowly in an unmarked car, were Markham and Knight. Markham drove, with Knight operating the camera. There wasn't a moment when he didn't snap a photo. Hobbes walked from the gardens towards the Bandstand, a small sheltered dome structure in the centre of the street. It was essentially the meeting point in Worthing. The car stopped, as Hobbes reached the Bandstand. Taking out his arms from his pockets, he very quickly left an envelope on a bench in the Bandstand, before then very briskly heading off in the direction of Montague Street, where there were no roads.
"He's heading up Montague Street, we'll have to head for the end of it and park somewhere until we see him." Markham then spun the car out of Liverpool Gardens.

Neither of the men saw Hobbes, who blocked their vision, drop the envelope. It was waiting, patiently, on the bench to be picked up.

Chapter Five
Caught In The Act

October 19th, a fog and mist covered evening across the breezy Worthing seafront. Outside the Dome Cinema, blending into the small crowd of people who had just seen a film, was Emerson. Keeping his low profile, he wore a hoodie. Every woman who left the cinema, he eyed up. Next to the Dome, however, was a loud and noisy pub. Emerson didn't want to go too close to a filled pub, in case he was recognised. It was 11:45PM, approaching midnight very soon. Emerson thought he wasn't being watched. He was wrong. Snatched by the shadows, on the seafront at a shelter with no working lights, was another hooded figure. Two hoodies would only add confusion to the chaos that was soon to erupt uncontrollably. Emerson's attention was hooked by a certain young woman, only just a woman, however. Simply a brunette with an amazing body, as Emerson saw it. To him, she was just an object. Stinking heavily of booze, he watched her cross the road from the pub, in tears, towards the darkened seafront. Wiping his lips on his sleeve, he began to follow his prey for its capture. The other hooded figure followed, but slowly, only waiting to pounce. The young woman was bawling her eyes out in a shelter on the seafront, on the side facing the pitch-black skies and sea.

"That fucking short skirt…" Emerson's slurred speech mumbled.

The woman bolted her head up in confusion, attempting to wipe away the floods of tears. "You what?"

"Damn, feisty… Angry. I like that you know…"

"Oh piss off, fucking twat…"

Emerson then grabbed her and threw her against the blurred glass of the shelter, to her absolute fear. Emerson's alcohol filled breath, whispering onto her soft, clear skin, leaving a trail of goose bumps. She was speechless in sheer fear.

"Mmm… Those golden thighs, darling. 30 odd years in prison, makes my blue balls the fucking… Fucking bluest ever." Emerson's grimy, disgusting hand began to lift up her short skirt. She was paralysed in fear, as he reached up and stuffed his hand in her knickers. As he was about to try, in his cockiness, to horrifically fist the young woman, a sudden shove sent Emerson flying to the ground. The other hooded man, who wore a black mask underneath, stood impressively over Emerson. He then kicked Emerson so hard in the chin, that his neck clicked and two teeth crumbled out. The hooded man then savagely punched Emerson repeatedly in the face, with the young woman hiding in the corner. Then, she felt her arm being softly grabbed.

"Run." The hooded figure muttered, before pulling the woman with him.

"Ugh…" Emerson struggled up in a bloody mess, watching the two head off towards the pier. Emerson grunted, before getting to his knees and, surprisingly quickly, heading for the road. Peering round the shelter, was Mark Hobbes, who was watching the hooded figure and the young woman speed off towards the bottom of the pier. He then shivered, and looked away to the ground.

"How could we have lost him!?" Markham shouted, as he began to turn the corner around Steyne Gardens towards the road between the Dome and the seafront. "He just ran into that crowd, there was like 20 of them at least. We'll just have to keep searching near pubs and shit, that crowd was outside one." Knight had his camera at the ready. As Markham then revved the engine and sped up hurriedly, out of nowhere the drunk Emerson, at the traffic lights, made a dash for the other side of the road.
"Shitting hell!" Markham roared, as he swerved to try and avoid Emerson. Emerson, however, swayed and fell into the speed of the car before Markham and he could properly react. The lard filled body came crashing onto the windscreen, even leaving a crack, before collapsing off the bonnet and onto the road. Markham stopped the car immediately, before hurrying out of the car with Knight, who urgently got out his radio.
Markham stopped above the unconscious Emerson. "It's him. Get an ambulance here, now!" Markham was much calmer and laid back, seeing that it was Emerson that he hit. "He was running from the seafront, something must be going on."

Hobbes then ran out into the street.
"Sir…" Knight was getting confused by the bombardment of suspects.
"Hey, hey! There's a body, underneath the pier!"
Both Markham and Knight halted.
"Another one! It's… It's horrible…" Hobbes broke off.
"Ralph, stay here." Markham followed Hobbes in the direction of the pier.

Waiting underneath the aging pier, in total darkness, was at first nothing. Markham couldn't see anything. He then took out his torch as he got closer to the pier, with Hobbes nervously watching, also looking around him. There was nobody else on the beach. Flicking the torch on, Markham gasped in shock and disappointment, that another innocent young woman had been slaughtered. And slaughtered, she certainly was. Her head was hanging on literally by a thread. Her ears had been chopped off and tossed aside onto the pebbles, with her abdomen laid neatly open by the killer, the bloody insides being shone upon by the moonlight. Although not as much of a disturbing sight as the other two victims, her face had been totally wrecked.

Come just after midnight, police had the street closed off, as Emerson was taken into an ambulance with Markham. Knight was with Heller, near the shelter, who was taking notes. Cowper stood with him, seeing the flashes of the camera, photographing the body, underneath the pier. Heller finished his note taking.

"What a fucking bizarre coincidence." He put his notebook away.

"So, we have two suspects, at the same place…" Cowper then took a look at Hobbes, who was being questioned in the street. "And he claims he found the body?"

"That's right sir. We lost him in Chatsworth Road near that nightclub, blended in with the crowd."

"Take him to the station for questioning, get him away from here Knight. We need to question him properly."

Knight nodded at Heller's request, before leaving.

"Some witnesses outside the Dome said they saw Emerson follow a young woman to the shelter, he had his hood up. But, they *then* saw another hoodie following. About a minute or two after, the young woman followed the hoodie towards the pier." Cowper referred to his notes.

"Did any of them see another man? A.k.a Hobbes."

"Not as far as I'm aware sir… But they were all wearing black hoodies, both of them."

Heller paced up and down, thoughtfully. "Got it. If there were only two, they are working together."

"You said 'if' sir?"

"Yep. This is the way I see it. We have Nathan Emerson, waiting outside the Dome to prey on a woman. He sees one, follows her up here. Then, we have another man, only a few yards away, who also follows. My guess is that this man beats Emerson up and takes the woman away, before killing her. Hobbes then claims to find the body."

"Your saying there's three people though? There were only two, Emerson and Hobbes."

"So, who was Hobbes? If nobody saw him, he must be the hooded man who followed Emerson. Right?"
Cowper nodded. "Exactly."
"Wrong. I say that nobody saw Hobbes, because he was already waiting on the other side of the shelter. That shelter has pillars, four of them, one in each corner. He could easily hide behind one so as not to be seen. I'm telling you Greg, Hobbes is working with the killer."
"So, he can't possibly be the killer?"
Heller shook his head. "Emerson certainly isn't the killer, but he is the only person other than Hobbes to come into close contact with him, I'm guessing. He'll be arrested and charged for sexual assault, but you handle questioning him. I'll deal with this."
"Right sir."
Heller then stood still in the breeze, watching the body underneath the pier. "From five witnesses' statements at that pub next to the Dome, they all said that she is 20-year-old Lucy Brown. Three victims, with a killer who disappears as quickly as he appears. Your typical murder mystery, eh?" Heller then patted Cowper on the shoulder, before leaving as he lit a cigarette.
"But where's the letter?" Cowper wandered, as Heller simply shrugged his shoulders.
"It'll pop up somewhere." Heller then went on his way.

Later that morning, around 2:00AM, a furious and now sober Emerson was waiting in the interview room. Then, Cowper entered with a police officer. Starting the tape and giving the essential details, before commencing.

"Nathan Emerson, you've been arrested for sexual assault on Lucy Brown, now deceased."
"You can't prove that I did a thing! She's dead, not like she's gonna leave you a statement or anything."
Cowper sighed. "When you were unconscious, and in hospital, from your known background Nathan, officers took a swab off of your fingers. We found Brown's DNA, specifically from her genital area. So, don't you dare try and lie to us."
Emerson was silenced.
"Now, let's get this out of the way. We know you aren't the Midnight Murderer, but what we do know is that you are one of the only people to see him and survive. So, we *need* every detail of what happened, and we need it now."
Emerson gulped. "Well, me and Lucy… Whatever her name is, were getting it on."
Cowper rolled his eyes. "I'm not in the mood for this."
Emerson nodded. "Then, some bloke attacked me, punched me. They both then ran down to the pier, to which I ran out of the shelter and got hit by one of you pigs!"
Cowper inhaled, unphased. "Mark Hobbes, he was on the seafront at the same time too. He says he didn't see you attacked at all. In fact, he says that you dragged Lucy to the pier, where you killed her, underneath, concealed in the darkness."
"It ain't fucking true! It ain't!"
"You still assaulted her! You also raped those four girls in 1986 to 1987. So explain to me why we should believe you!?"
"Because I didn't kill anyone before!"

"Before now?"
Emerson hesitated. "Where's the proof? Eh!?"
"For which of the offenses?"
"Alright, alright… I did assault her, but barely. But kill her… I didn't, alright? I didn't."
Cowper squinted, focusing on the careless Emerson.

The bloody body, wrapped up in a body bag, was being carried by four officers from underneath the pier. It was taken into the back of an ambulance. A few small crowds were being held back, intrigued in seeing the body. Also standing near the crowds was Heller, who was standing quietly with Stubbs.
"So, what does the letter say?" Stubbs wasn't even in his usual, annoying journalist mode.
"Haven't found it yet. We've searched the beach, the seafront. Nothing yet."
"Maybe he left it in like… Like a bottle? Bottle messages in the sea?"
Heller turned. "Clever idea, Stubbs. But no. Her wants us to find it, after searching though. He wouldn't risk it going in the sea."
Stubbs nodded. Then, Heller gravely turned at the ambulance, where the body bag had been loaded inside. He then grabbed Stubbs, before hurrying over through the crowds and over to the ambulance.
"Wait!" Heller shouted. Stubbs joined him, to which Heller opened the body bag. "Close those doors Stubbs!" Stubbs slammed the doors shut. Heller showed his warrant badge to the officer inside, before zipping open the bag. Stubbs shivered at the harrowing sight. Heller

then put on his white gloves and took a pair of tongs from his coat.

"Inspector, why have you brought me here?"

"Because, Eddie. The paper is known to be all lay with the facts, ever since the new management took over. You practically ass lick your bosses, barely print any detail about these murders. Cause you see, many people think that, if the police haven't caught the Midnight Murderer by now, why should we listen to their warnings about being alone at night, all that kinda shit…" Heller gently put the tong inside the vagina, with a shocked Stubbs looking on. "Maybe, if you see the injuries first hand, you might…" Heller took out a bloody envelope, making Stubbs gag. "Print the truth. The more women know about what this killer does, the more cautious they'll be." Heller then opened the envelope, but there was no polaroid.

"Stubbs, if you get a letter, don't open it. Bring it to us immediately, because the killer took a polaroid, but didn't have time for it to print."

Stubbs got closer to Heller. "What does the letter say?" Heller began.

"**To Sussex Police,**

What a great hiding place, eh? Sorry if the letters a little wet. I'm nowhere near done. All this, the murders, its fun! I have no real motive, just the fact that its fun! Besides, it gives you a job to do

```
Detective Inspector Heller. You've got
an almost clean record. But have you
met your match? With each slaying,
someone will get framed, whilst
someone walks away to kill again.
Sorry for the unenthusiastic letter,
but I couldn't really think of much
else to say, other than the fact that
I'm really enjoying the chase.

Best of luck,
The Midnight Murderer"
```

Heller slammed the letter with a grimaced look onto the table. The ambulance sirens began to wail as it went on it's way. Stubbs was chilled to the bone by Heller's silence. Stubbs looked around the ambulance.
"So, why am I still here?"
"Your gonna print everything that you see this morning. The people of Worthing *need* to know that this isn't just a fun mystery for the police to try and solve, it's real, it's fucking real. And it isn't gonna end any time soon."
The two men looked down from the body in total silence.

Cowper sat with his heavy head in his hands, yawning. Then, Knight entered.
"Sir, where's Heller?"
Cowper glanced up with cloudy eyes. "He's… He's gone to the hospital."
"No letter yet?"

Cowper shook his head. He then looked in his notebook. "Hobbes has shaved, did you notice that?"

"Didn't really pay particular attention to it to be honest."

"Really? Well hear this. Emerson and two other people, who saw another hooded man in the street, say they could see his mouth and nose very clearly. Our killer's had a shave."

Knight shrugged his shoulders. "I mean it is very odd, Hobbes being there at the same time as the killer."

"Hmm, *very*."

Green then entered, a solemn look about him. He slammed the door shut. "Where is Heller?"

"The hospital sir, he radioed me a few minutes ago."

"Well, I'm guessing it was his fucking stupid idea to spy on Hobbes?"

Cowper got up. "Sir?"

"Don't play stupid with me Cowper. You, PC Knight, and Sergeant Markham, were watching Mark Hobbes. And believe me, I know. I've heard both their statements Detective, so don't try and lie to me."

"Look sir, you are briefed all the time. You know all the evidence against Hobbes, it was only right to try this out."

"Okay." Green sarcastically agreed, before taking a chair and sitting in it, crossing his legs expectantly. "And did you catch him in the act Knight?"

Knight began to stutter like a nervous school pupil doing a class presentation. "Erm… No, sir. We lost him."

Green shook his head. "I'm recalling it."

"No sir, you can't!"

"You'll do as I say!" Green snapped, banging his fist onto Heller's desk. The two officers were left in obedient silence.

"And you can tell Heller that if he doesn't agree, he can take it up with me and the PCC."

"Yes sir…" Cowper had glued gritted teeth, as Green nodded and left, slamming the door shut again. Cowper then bolted to the laptop, opening it and instantly typing away.

"What're you doing sir?"

"Emailing the Police and Crime Commissioner, see what she has to say about this."

"But sir, he said the Commissioner was on his side pretty much!"

"I think he's bluffing." Cowper was typing away angrily. He then stopped.

"What's up?"

"Emerson. We'll have to drop the charges for murder. Another team is going to handle the sexual assault investigation, which we will assist with when we can. In the meantime, he'll stay here."

Knight nodded. "Should I tell Heller? About what Green said."

Cowper shook his head. "He's in a bad enough mood, we'll wait till he's back."

Outside the hospital, in the crisp cold dark night, Heller was puffing on his fourth cigarette. Stubbs felt awkward, but remained.

"Heller, can I ask you something?"

"Go for it." Heller stared at Stubbs.

"Well, do you think you'll get him? The Midnight Murderer?"

Heller smiled, but then pondered. "I wish I knew. We've got some of the best of Sussex Police working on this case, day and night, 24/7. But this twisted killer is clever. Yeah, he's a local, very close to those we've previously and still suspect, and manages to frame them. This is one tough fucking cookie. And he'll keep doing it, and keep killing, till he's caught."

Stubbs nodded. "I take it he doesn't intend to get caught?"

"Correct. To be honest, I just don't know if we'll get the bastard. Print that if you like, but he's nearly cleverer than the entire team working on the murders put together."

Stubbs looked hopeless, as did Heller. Heller then stood firmly onto the cigarette butt on the ground, putting his hands deep in his coat pockets. "You see, it's also pretty difficult with Green breathing down our necks."

"Superintendent Green?"

"Yep. He has authority over any case he wants, as does the Commissioner. It's not long till he finds out that we had a surveillance team on one of our suspects, which he'll put an end to."

Stubbs was frowning in total confusion. "But why would he do that? Surely it's a good idea?"

Heller scoffed softly. "He's a tight ass, money this, money that. You see I put two officers working on the case onto it, so not a proper equipment filled operation, just spying on the suspect armed with only an unmarked car and a camera. So, it doesn't cost any money, just

deep down, I think Green wants the murders to go unsolved."
Stubbs' eyes bulged out in shock.
"If they go uncaught, he'll get more money to fund the case through the years. But most of that money, will be going straight in his wallet, the high ups none the wiser. He's always been like this, ever since he became Superintendent in 2008."
"Isn't there an anti-corruption unit or something?"
"Yes, but they'd rely on evidence, which we don't have."
Stubbs stared deep into Heller's eyes, with a worried and very concerned look about him. "So, he, dictates the case? And if the killings go unsolved, it's his fault?"
Heller, with slightly watery eyes, nodded.
"Then don't you dare, Inspector, don't you *dare* let him dictate the case. Now you do what you have to do to catch this killer, that's me… Me asking as a scared member of the public, please, please catch him Heller!"
The hushed but urgent whisper from the journalist totally silenced Heller, who sniffed. He then nodded. "Anyway, let's get the mortuary over and done with shall we?"
Heller and Stubbs then made their way towards the automatic double doors of the hospital. As soon as they opened and both men placed even one foot inside the reception, they were attacked, invaded and bombarded by the media. Retina burning flashes from cameras, constant questions poking away at Heller and an entire mob blocking the way for both men.
"Fuck sake!"
One police officer heard Heller, as he leapt straight to Heller.
"How the hell did they get here?"

"They guessed you'd come here after you got in the ambulance, got in via the children's section."
Heller nodded. "Right, well we need to get to the mortuary
Constable, so let's get them the fuck outta our way!"
Both officers smiling like misbehaving children, Stubbs tagged along as Heller and the officer shoved the crowd with all their strength out the way. As they ploughed through, Stubbs squeezed through and hit the lift button, to which the doors opened instantly.
"Heller!"
Heller followed Stubbs' cry, as he and the officer got into the lift with Stubbs. Before long, Heller had pressed the -2 floor button, and the doors had closed.
In the chilling mortuary, Heller was with Stubbs. Cuthbertson was hovering over the body, that was laid neatly on the metal table.
"So, what's this development that you want to show us?"
Cuthbertson scratched his chin. "Ah, yes, yes… Well it's not as horrific as the injuries that the victims usually get, but it's a bloody dreadful sight to see."
Cuthbertson began to turn the body over. Heller jumped to his aid, as they turned the naked body onto the front. Heller practically retreated from what he saw. Carved with great difficulty into her back, were the words "BACK STABBER".
"Jesus!" Stubbs felt like he was going to throw up.
"Awful, quite awful."
Heller observed the injuries. "Clearly, she still had her clothes on, I mean they were still on when her body was found."

"How long between that Emerson fellow being knocked down and the body being discovered?"
Heller still scanned the body. "About… Two minutes at least. This guy is fucking showing off."
"Nearly impossible, right? But it's been so poorly yet perfectly carved in, took at least… Thirty seconds I guess."
"Oh, come on!" Heller couldn't digest this.
"Well, her face isn't as mutilated as the others. Takes the killer at least ten seconds to chop off the ears, maybe another thirty or so to rip open the abdomen. Then he simply stabs the body randomly till he flees, didn't have time to complete the job."
Stubbs gagged as he left the room.
"I take it this has been photographed and recorded?"
"Yes Inspector."
Heller then paced up to Cuthbertson, talking in murmurs. "So, doctor… I couldn't help but realise you were very accurate about how long it would have taken the killer to perform the injuries on the victim?"
"Well…" Cuthbertson was almost avoiding the question. "Yes, well, it was just an opinion from a medical professional."
Cuthbertson nervously began to wash his hands at the sink.
"So, who do you think is behind the murders?"
"Not really for me to say, to be honest. You stick to your job, I'll stick to mine."
Heller then crept up behind the doctor. "I think it would help us, Doctor Cuthbertson."
Cuthbertson turned the taps off, staring at the wall and not turning.

"Well. From how quickly these injuries were performed, I'd say a doctor maybe." Cuthbertson turned, smirking. "Typical murder story, eh? The killer *must* have medical, or rough anatomical knowledge, to do something like this."

"A typical Jack the Ripper copycat."

"There hasn't been a Jack the Ripper copycat, Inspector. I'd hardly call Jack the Stripper a copycat, you know… The Hammersmith Nudes."

"I'm aware of them. But you see these programmes and films about Ripper copycats, and sometimes, that pops up somewhere, about the medical knowledge."

Cuthbertson abruptly headed for the doors.

"One more thing doctor..."

Cuthbertson sighed in exasperation, eager to leave. "What?"

"Where were you between 11:00PM yesterday evening and 12:30AM this morning?"

"How dare you." Cuthbertson spat.

"Avoiding the question doesn't make you look any better." Heller took out his notebook and pen.

"Fine." Cuthbertson sighed again. "Here, just doing my job. Examining a man who died of a heart attack yesterday."

Heller nodded. "Okay, that's all, you can go now."

Cuthbertson then hurried out of the mortuary, passing a recovering Stubbs. Shortly after, Heller too left the mortuary.

"He left very eagerly." Stubbs noted.

"Trying to get away from me and my questions."

"Hey! Do you suspect him?"

Heller patted Stubbs on the shoulder. "I'm going to find a security guard, have a look at some tapes. I suggest you get down to some writing Mr. Herald."
Heller then left Stubbs alone in the darkened corridor.

Later that morning, the sun was breaking through the morning clouds. In the bustling town centre, Heller and Cowper had just got some coffee from Starbucks. Travelling down South Street, they were deep in conversation.
"I knew he'd do this, and we both know why." Heller wasn't the least bit surprised.
"I briefed the team on the only changes to the killer, he shaved, and this time didn't change clothes at all, but still had a backpack."
Heller saw, directly ahead on the other side of the street, a man with a woolly hat. The man, in his mid-twenties at least, was also drinking coffee and standing in the door frame of a closed shop. The eyes were grappled onto Heller.
"Green could do a little better though, couldn't he?"
"What'd you mean James?"
Heller nodded his head in the direction of the man.
Cowper took a glance ahead, immediately noticing the young man.
"I see what you mean."
"Now *we* are being watched, to make sure we don't track down Hobbes. But you'd think our woolly officer would try and blend in a bit, sticking out like a sore thumb."
"I suppose Knight and Markham are going to be watched too."

Heller nodded in agreement.
"Heller, I've had a thought. It's October 20th, 11 days till Halloween."
"Oh, right. You suggesting we go to the annual party as a double act down at Bettison's?"
"No, nothing like that. I'm thinking the killer is gonna strike again, on Halloween. Think about it, it would be the perfect time. Creepy, scary Halloween, scaring that day permanently."
"Well, I agree with you. Until then, we'll have to put another suspect down."
"Who?"
Heller took out five photographs, from a CCTV camera, from his coat.
"These images are from Worthing Hospital, at the reception yesterday evening and early this morning, do you recognise him?"
Cowper took the photos as he and his partner sat down on a bench outside the Guilbourne Centre, a shabby and cheap shopping centre in the heart of Worthing. Cowper studied every image.
"It… It looks like, Doctor Cuthbertson?"
"That's right. I asked him where he was between 11:00PM on October 19th and 12:30AM this morning. He said he was at the mortuary the whole time."
"Well, clearly not. But why did you ask him?"
"He estimated the exact amount of time it would have taken the Midnight Murderer to perform the injuries on Lucy Brown."
"Right. But I doubt it was him James."
"Then why lie about where he was?"

A few days had passed along, no progress. For Hobbes, each passing day kept him from his sleep, from eating, from drinking, even from leaving his home. He hadn't received any texts from the killer, until 10:45AM, October 28th. Hobbes' phone pinged with a text tone, as he hurried from the kitchen back to the living room, leaving his unfinished tea. Unlocking his phone, the text simply ordered:

"Answer the door."

Thundering from the outside door, which led into the hallway of the flats, was a firm and urgent knock. Hobbes peered through the white curtains, to see the sleeve of a man waiting at the door. Hobbes inhaled sharply, and grabbed a nearby knife and tightly gripped onto it, the blade pointing accusingly towards the window. Throwing the curtains aside and quickly opening the window and jumped out. Standing in the door way, with a thick winter coat and warm woolly hat, was Jeffrey Stevens.

Chapter Six
Treading On Thin Ice

Hobbes nervously passed an equally nervous Stevens a mug of coffee, Stevens instantly grabbing it and gulping it endlessly.
"So, what the hell is going on? Eh!?" Hobbes was very impatient.
"Look, look, before you start on me, I'm not the Midnight Murderer…" Stevens said in a mocking mystery voice. He slammed the mug onto the table and laid back in the cold leather sofa.
"Then why are you here? You must have been texting me, telling me to open the door!"
Stevens got out his phone and got up his text messages, from the killer. "Here. I've even named the contact after

him. I've only just started getting messages, like you have too I'm guessing."

Hobbes was scanning the texts, there weren't many, and they only were the killer saying who he was and that Stevens had to go to Hobbes' house, or Hobbes would be framed for the next murder.

"You're a mate, I couldn't risk having him framing you for the next murder."

"But… If the police see that text, then any evidence against me on the next murder, they'll know it'll be fake."

Stevens looked unimpressed. "He has my watch, must have got it off me when I was drunk without me noticing. Seems we've got to work together." Stevens took back his phone, typing away on it.

Hobbes took out his phone after getting a text.

"Is it him?"

Hobbes sat down, next to Stevens. "Mark, Jeffrey. You will both soon be released from my blackmail chain, but only after you assist me. Wait until October 31st, where you will meet in Victoria Park after I text you both."

Stevens took Hobbes' phone and took a long hard look at the text. "Shit… So, it's just a waiting game till then?"

"I… I guess."

The men were now standing in silence.

"I don't like the idea of helping this guy… It's fucked up, and we're just gonna get thrown into the deep end by him."

Hobbes broke out of another trance. "Eh?"

"Face it Mark! He's just saying he'll stop the blackmail to get us to corporate. He will literally make it look like we are the bad guys and stop the killings."

"You don't know that! This has been eating away at me ever since Jessica Powell was fucking slaughtered in those woods! I can't get sleep, I can't eat... I can't leave the fucking house unless he tells me too, and he's only done that once!"

"Alright, alright, calm down... Look, of course I'll do this. But only to help you out man, this is only gonna go tits up for the both of us."

Hobbes was beginning to lose his temper. "I want to be free! And I *will* be!"

"Fine, I get that. But as far as I'm concerned Mark, even *you* could be the killer."

Hobbes squared up threateningly to Stevens. "As could *you* be."

Stevens shook his head and sighed, before nodding awkwardly as if to say bye to Hobbes, before leaving the flat.

Moments before Stevens and Hobbes' encounter, Heller was walking on the outskirts of the town centre, in West Worthing. Sensing for the duration of the journey so far, Heller was being followed by two officers in an unmarked car. He then took up his phone and called Cowper. Cowper answered in an instant.

"Cowper, Heller here."

"Yes... I know, you don't need to say your name whenever you answer James, I've saved your contact you dope."

"Right, well. I'm in Tarring Road, got some officers tracking me."

"Well what are you doing in West Worthing? That's close to Hobbes you know."

"Of course I do, that's why I'm here. I have your house keys, you live in Harrow Road, right?"

"Yes… Why?"

Heller took out some house keys from his pocket as he began to approach Harrow Road. "Because I've got your house keys."

Cowper paused over the phone. "What?!"

"Yep, if I run and quickly sneak into your house, then I can get out the back way after I lose them."

"But… James, how did you-"

"Never mind, just thought I'd tell you. We need to keep watching Hobbes."

Heller hung up before Cowper could reply. Then, after a few seconds hesitation, Heller barrelled into Harrow Road. The car, stuck in traffic, was held in place. The officers inside were barking into the radios and trying to look out for Heller, who was quite a fast runner. As they pair of officers began to get out of the car, Heller got to 23 Harrow Road and in the blink of an eye, was inside. The officers were out, looking ahead into Harrow Row. Realising they were defeated, they got back inside the car.

Heller had soon reached Victoria Park, where he stood behind a tree, not even trying to hide himself. Filming on his phone, Heller's face dropped in surprise as Stevens left the flats. Hobbes was watching through the curtains in the window. Stevens then walked back towards the park, neither he nor Hobbes seeing Heller.

Cowper was watching the footage at the station. He, too, was in shock.

"Two people involved in the case, seeing each other. Odd right?" Heller then sat down in his seat at his desk. "But that fucking Superintendent can't know about this, okay? Or that's us off the case, and I can't afford to lose this case."

Cowper nodded. "Anyway, about Mark Hobbes and Jeffrey Stevens. You do realise that they are friends, or must be? They usually frequent that pub where we arrested Hall."

Heller muttered to himself, before Green entered with the two officers who were attempting to track down Heller earlier.

"Heller." Green was, as usual, unimpressed. "I have a bone to pick with you."

"Oh, go ahead…" Heller simply continued to read through papers and documents.

"Detective Inspector! I expect more respect from you!"

Heller nodded uninterestingly.

"I would rather like to know why you ran away from these two officers?"

"Well, I could tell I was being followed. So, I ran."

"Why!?"

Heller got to his feet. "I would like to conduct this investigation without being followed. Besides, surely you shouldn't even be telling me all this?"

"Heller, I would seriously watch it if I were you. Your treading on *very* thin ice."

"And you are in *very* hot water, Superintendent. I'm going to conduct this investigation how I like, so you can go ahead and get all the surveillance you on me that you can afford, but it won't stop me doing this in my own way."

Green's lips were trembling in anger. "You have two chances left, Heller. You are one of the best detectives we have, but if you keep acting like a loose cannon, I will personally remove you from the case."

Green then headed for the door.

"I know you don't want this case solved." Heller murmured.

The entire room was filled with an ominous silence. Green didn't turn around. "Everyone, out. Now."

Cowper hesitantly followed the two officers, with him and Heller quickly sharing a glance, before the door closed.

"You better watch that tongue of yours James. What the devil makes you think you can go around saying things like that!?"

"Worried that you can't keep your cool, sir?"

"It won't be solved, Heller. You lot can't find him, and you never will. It's a lost cause."

"Exactly, and that's down to you. Cutting the surveillance, *wanting* someone who's innocent to get charged for it."

"Is that all? Ha! Thought you could come up with better lies than that."

Heller then sat down, indicating the chair opposite his desk. Green slowly sat down.

"The reason why I don't trust you, is because of Raph Thomas."

"What about him? I mean, that case went unsolved."
"No it fucking didn't! And you know it! After that, that case… It ruined my life, fucked it up completely… And that's all down to *you*!"
Green smiled mockingly, shaking his head.
"So, trust me, I'm gonna solve this case, even if it's the fucking end of me. You won't stand in my way, and this case is certainly gonna be the end of you, sir."
"What're you talking about?" Green was even laughing. Heller rose from his seat. "Because I care about Worthing, I care about West Sussex. I grew up here, I have a love for this place, and the people here. So I'm not gonna let this killer scar Worthing, I'm gonna bring him down, me and Cowper, and the team we have. And when I do, all the truth will spill out, and you'll be fucking finished sir!"
Green got up to respond, but Heller was already out of the office. Green genuinely looked a little concerned, but not too much. He then took out his phone and dialled a number, as he approached the blinds at the windows overlooking Chatsworth Road. Outside, an army of people were roaring away in bitterness, anger and almost hatred. All this, however, was bred out of fear. This was becoming an everyday thing outside the station.
The other end answered the call. "Yes, hello Commissioner. I think we need to discuss Detective Inspector James Heller, and a replacement for him, urgently."

Heller was with Cowper, in the busy and steaming hot canteen in the station. Waiting for Cowper, the pair then carried their trays and sat next to a window which overlooked the Post Office building and the Connaught Theatre.

"Early lunch?" Cowper started to fill his mouth with creamy chicken tikka masala.

"Yep. Gave Green a piece of my mind, told him that when we catch the killer, it'll be his downfall."

Cowper was impressed, nodding along. "Hmm. Well done man, hope that won't mean you get struck off the case?"

Heller shook his head cluelessly as he bit into his big fat burger.

"So, I think we should probably talk about Halloween." Cowper began. "I reckon the killer is gonna kill again, on that night. We both think that."

"What day is Halloween this year?"

"Tuesday…" Cowper tried to make out what Heller said as he talked with his mouth full. "I say, we try and lose the squads that are gonna be watching us. We need to follow Hobbes and Stevens."

"What makes you think that?" Heller may as well have been talking fluent Cantonese.

"Huh?"

Heller swallowed the bite of his burger. "What makes you think that?"

"Them both meeting, before Halloween. If one of them is the killer, then they were arranging the next murder, but a double act. Both will be at the scene of the killing."

"And if they are both being blackmailed, a similar thing." Heller put his burger down, thinking and thinking. "How will we be able to trace Stevens?"

"We have his address. Well, I took it from him… Not procedure, given the fact he only gave us information, but I thought it would come in handy. Call it gut instinct, take anyone's' address who is involved in the case."
Heller smiled joyfully. "Damn, that's good thinking. Where does he live?"
"Some flats in Grand Avenue, Cardinal Court."
The men then became very hushed.
"What do you think we should do Greg?"
"Erm… Well, I'll stay at the station, in case Green goes snooping around. You watch Hobbes, Knight could watch… Robert Hall?"
"Why Hall?"
"To definitely exclude him from the list of suspects. Then, have Markham watch Stevens."
Heller grabbed Cowper's hand. They then shook on it.
"It's a plan!" Heller then got back into his burger.
Cowper, full of modesty, got back to his curry.

Chapter Seven
The Two Killers

October 31st, Halloween. It was approaching 8:30PM, the majority of children were now home, with the older kids still out trick or treating and the Halloween parties only just starting. Victoria Park was shadowed by the darkness of the night sky, but illuminated gently by the full moon. Waiting near a tree opposite his flat, Hobbes was waiting in anticipation for Stevens. To his near delight, Stevens tapped him from behind, making him jump.
"Never thought I'd say I'm glad to see you." Hobbes tried to warm up his hands by blowing into them.

"I've got news for you…" Stevens opened his backpack and took out Hobbes' missing disposable camera. "The killer, left this at my doorstep."
Hobbes couldn't believe it. "Give it here!" Hobbes reached for the camera, before getting into a tangled struggle with Stevens.
"Fucking hell, let go!" Stevens threw his fist right into Hobbes' face, causing him to fall to the ground. Stevens was panting, before helping Hobbes up. "I'm sorry mate, but you can't have it, or we'll be made to look like the Midnight Murderers, okay?"
Hobbes nodded, wiping the blood that was pouring from his nose. Stevens took out a tissue and handed it to his friend.
"Anyway, you heard anything?"
"Yes…" Hobbes was breathing shakily in fear. "I had to cut out a clump of my hair, wear this winter hat, and that's all."
"I know why you've had to do that. He wants you to leave it at the second murder site, tonight."
"Whoa whoa whoa… What!? Second murder site?"
"I'm afraid so. He's gonna kill outside of Worthing, then again in Worthing. I've gotta go to Barnham, leave this camera there."
"But then I'm going to look guilty anyway!"
"The police already know that you got your disposable camera stolen, so don't worry."
"So… We're both going to meet him. The Midnight Murderer…"
Stevens gravely nodded. Hobbes sniffed, before nodding. "Good luck then…" Hobbes held out his hand.

"Good luck man." Stevens shook Hobbes' hand, before turning and hurrying away for Worthing train station. Hobbes simply went back into his flat and locked the door, firmly.

"Right then!" Heller closed the door of his office. Inside, gathered, were Cowper, Markham and Knight. "Knight and Markham, you're not off duty tonight."
"Eh? But… We are?" Knight took of his police cap.
"Not anymore. Now you two have been followed before, right?"
Markham and Knight nodded.
"Well, they're gonna be watching us. All of us. But we're gonna have to lose them, in any way possible."
"Sir, what's going on?" Markham scratched his head in confusion.
"Mark Hobbes and Jeffrey Stevens have met up, and we have reason to believe that they're gonna either kill someone tonight, or assist in the killing of someone tonight. We have video evidence of them meeting in Hobbes' flat."
"I see. And what's the reason for you thinking that sir?"
"Gut instinct Markham." Heller answered before Cowper. "Here's what we'll be doing. You, Knight, will be staying here with Cowper to cover for Markham and myself."
"Wait, I thought he was gonna be watching Hall?"
"No need. The more people here, the better and less suspicious it'll look. Markham, you'll be keeping an eye on Jeffrey Stevens, and I'll be watching Hobbes. Okay?"
Markham and Cowper nodded.

"Do we get paid overtime for this?" Knight curiously asked.
"No." Heller then opened the door. "Markham, head for Cardinal Court, Grand Avenue. That's where Stevens lives."
"Right sir. But, how should I lose the surveillance team?"
"Well… I dunno. Now off you go, keep me informed!" Heller then pushed Markham out of the office. "We'll be off then."
"Best of luck James." Cowper said with nervousness.
Heller nodded with a smile at Cowper, before closing the door behind him. Knight then turned to Cowper.
"What should I do sir?"
Cowper threw his phone to Knight, which he caught.
"Call up a good Chinese takeaway, get me a chicken curry and chicken chow Mein."
Before Knight could protest, Cowper was typing away at the laptop.
"Have you heard back from the Commissioner?"
"Not yet." Cowper shared Knight's worry.

In Barnham, a small village in West Sussex near Chichester, was only filled with the mumbled noises of party music in houses across the village. A drunken Megan Lewis was muttering and slurring to herself as she stopped in front of the ramp at Barnham railway station, which led up to platform 3. Lewis had been waiting on platform 1, until she realised she had to get to platform 3 in order to get home to Brighton. The station, at 11:45PM, was empty. Only two people were also there, but were right on the other side of the station to

Lewis. As she finally mountaineered the ramp and got onto the platform, she could only see a blur, then clear vision, then back to blurriness and so on. The entire station, bar the passing trains, was dead. The orange lights of the arrival board were nearly dead, with only one more train coming from Southampton to Brighton, in ten minutes. Lewis dropped her bottle, which came crashing down onto the concrete platform. Looking around to see if she caught anyone's attention, she only saw the tracks leaving the station briefly, before being faded and tucked away by the pitch black ahead. Turning around, she came face to face with Jeffrey Stevens. Stevens was smiling in a friendly manner. Immediately, Lewis' hair caught his gaze. Long sweeping blonde hair, a short but petite young woman, everything about her looked beautiful, until Stevens saw her sad face. She had been crying, which had washed away her make-up.
"Evening. Happy Halloween!" Stevens chuckled.
"Happ… Christmas…" Lewis turned then fell onto the bench next to her. Stevens looked around quickly, and seeing that he and Lewis were on a bench far reaching towards the end of the platform, he was satisfied and worriedly sat down beside Lewis.
"Been partying hard, eh?" Stevens laughed nervously.
"Go away… Don't talk to strangers…" Lewis then cried out in teary laughter, burying her head onto Stevens' lap. She was then as silent as a mouse. Stevens sighed, as he tapped his feet. He was waiting for someone.
"You erm… You waiting for the 11:55? To Brighton?" Lewis replied in a mumble.
"Hey, I'm just gonna… Gonna go to the toilet, I'll be right back, okay?"

Lewis was snoring, having now sprawled herself onto the bench after Stevens got up. Darting his eyes around him once more, Stevens then took out a small baseball bat from his bag. Without hesitation, he clubbed Lewis with a cringeworthy crack of the head. Making sure he was out of view of cameras on the platform once again, he put the bat back in his backpack, then picked up Lewis. Quickly, he ran onto the train tracks very carefully, then jumping onto the grassy knoll beside the tracks. He then placed the body carefully onto the tracks, before taking one last look around him. Stevens then ran back towards the station in panic, but once he was there, he sat down on another bench in front of the café, out of view of the tracks, trying to erase what he had just done from his memory. However, he couldn't resist, and took another look at the tracks.

Heller had managed to disguise himself as a uniformed officer, to evade the surveillance team outside the station. Keeping his head drawn low, he was waiting behind some bushes in Victoria Park, keeping a look out on Hobbes' flat. The curtains were drawn, but the orange glow told Heller that the lights were on. Oddly, he hadn't heard a peep from Markham since they left the station. Until now, that was. His phone started vibrating, and it was Markham. Unblinking and still watching the house, Heller answered.
"Markham! Where have you been?"
"Sir, I've only just managed to get service. I'm on the train."
"But why are you calling me?"

"Green could be monitoring the radios, but anyway. Stevens left his apartment, about 10:00PM. He hopped on a train about half an hour later, which I just about missed. I had to wait till the next train to Southampton, which I'm on."

"He's not going to Southampton, it's not in West Sussex. I'd say he's going as far as… Chichester. Stop off at Chichester or Barnham, try and find some station staff. They might be able to tell you where he went."

"Hmm, maybe. I'm heading for Barnham, just left Ford."

"Keep me informed."

"Yes sir." Markham then hung up.

"Come on you bastard… What're you up to?" Heller was biting his lip as he watched the still and silent flat.

Markham was waiting on a lonely train, in an empty carriage.

"We are now approaching Barnham." The clear female voice announced, but all Markham could see was pitch black outside. The passing four minutes felt like four hours, before Markham saw some faint light. It was the dimming lights of Barnham station, as the train began to slow down. Immediately, Markham spotted Stevens panting on the platform opposite him. As the train continued moving, Markham passed into the next carriage to watch Stevens, but after the train stopped, Markham's vision was obscured by another train slowing down, the Brighton train.

"Shit!" Markham then turned and hammered on the button to open the train doors. After several beeps, the doors opened. The cold breeze of the winter night shoved

Markham full force into his face. The uniformed officer then rushed past the railing and then down the ramp below the tracks, desperate to get to platform 3. As he climbed up the ramp and got onto platform 3, he heard the familiar beeping of the doors, which were literally about to close. The officer then reached for the doors, which closed. He was then face to face with a surprised and confused Stevens. Stevens swore he could recognise the man, but didn't have time to put his finger on it, as his train began moving along, with Markham standing alone on the platform. Taking his cap off and throwing it to the ground in disgust, Markham then realised that there were no more trains going to and leaving Barnham. "Fucking… Fuck sake!"

The station was pretty quiet, surprising considering the number of parties there usually were at Halloween. Cowper was on his fifth coffee, as he held his tired head in his hand. He was writing and writing away, with Knight looking through several files in the filing cabinets.
"Sir, how much longer do I have to pretend to look at these files?"
"Till I say so Ralph, we need to make sure Green doesn't get suspicious."
Then, on cue, Green entered the office without a knock.
"Evening Inspector." Green said, in grimace.
"Evening sir." Was the miserable response.
Green looked around the office, and noticed Knight taking a huge amount of interest in the files. "So… Where's DI Heller?"

Cowper yawned, only to give him a few seconds to think of a response. "Out taking a look around the streets sir."
"Why?"
"He's just out and about, trying to see if he'll spot the killer. Think he's more towards East Worthing, that's where most of the parties are."
"Idiot, he'll stand more chance of a fucking plane crashing here than catching the killer! Well, when he's back, tell him I need to have a word with him will you?"
"Of course sir."
"Thank you." Green then surveyed the room. "Expecting him to strike tonight? Halloween, making his mark on the holiday."
"Yes, but usually he'd kill around now, its…" Cowper checked his watch. "11:58PM. Typically, someone will find the body within half an hour or an hour after."
"So, it's just a waiting game then eh?"
Cowper nodded. The room was left in an awkward silence. Knight watched his back, as he saw Green sit down in the chair opposite the desk. Then, Cowper's radio crackled. All eyes turned onto the radio, as Cowper picked it up. After a pause, Cowper spoke into the radio.
"Cowper here."
There was a brief static.
"Markham here sir, I've… I've found a body, at Barnham train station."
Everyone frowned in confusion.
"Barnham?"
"Yes sir, on the tracks."
"Right, we'll get everyone there. Stay with the body Sergeant." Cowper stuffed the radio into his pocket. "Knight, get a patrol car ready."

"What in the name of fuck was Markham doing in Barnham? He's off duty."
Cowper grabbed his coat and put it on. "Long story sir, we'll explain later."
"I don't like the sound of this…" Green was growing suspicious.
"Then don't listen." Cowper remarked as he took out his radio again and followed Knight into the hallway outside. "James, body found, Barnham railway station. Where are you?"
Green watched from the office as Cowper and Knight disappeared. He crossed his arms and inhaled with a bitter look about him.

By 12:35AM, the whole of Barnham station was now filled with police presence. Heller and Cowper stood over the mutilated body of Megan Lewis, lying pretty much where Stevens had left her. Her head had been cut off, and as usual, the face and abdomen had been mutilated. Her clothes had been taken off and her genitals looked like a splattered, messy painting by a child. Her legs were left up, almost indicating that she had been sexually assaulted.
"Why Barnham?" Heller wandered, as he looked at the body with sadness.
"Heller!" Green cried. Heller and Cowper turned to see the figure of Green blocking the large lights on the tracks. Green ran to the detective. "What the hell are you playing at!? Do you want me to replace you or something?"
"Sir?" Heller feigned confusion.

"You know what I'm on about. You and Markham were doing your own little surveillance operation, weren't you?"
Heller nodded. "Yes, we were. And I take responsibility for him. I'm his superior, he was acting under orders."
"You little shit!" Green nearly went for Heller, before being held back by Cowper. "Me and the Commissioner will be meeting very soon, to discuss letting you go!"
"Well, until then, leave me to do my job, yeah?" Heller turned back to take a look at the body.
"I'll be speaking about taking you off the case too Cowper."
"Yes sir." Cowper beamed with sarcasm. Green, furious, turned and walked off back towards the station. "We checked out the CCTV between 11:45AM and just after midnight, nothing at all was seen. But, Markham was seen giving chase to a man who got onto a train, bound for Brighton."
Heller turned to face the station, specifically platform 3. "The killer must have been with her over there. There's a smashed bottle there, she must have been drunk, or she was bottled. I mean look at the injuries on her head."
Lewis lay silent and undisturbed.
"She couldn't have been aware of what was happening, the others weren't drunk. Her eyes are open, she must have woken up as the attack was happening…" Heller knelt beside Lewis, about to tuck her hair back out of her face, before stopping, realising that he couldn't.
"She couldn't have done anything, she must have been paralytic." Cowper shared the sadness.
"Her mouth was covered." Heller then took another regretful look at Lewis. "I'm so sorry…"

There was a long silence after, before Heller got back up with several clicks from his aching body. Markham then walked over to the two detectives.

"Given my statement sir, Green is less than impressed." Markham sighed.

"Yes, we know. So, you saw Stevens get on a train that was bound for Brighton?"

"Yes sir."

"Well, if he left just at midnight..." Heller then ran back to the platform, with the confused Cowper and Markham joining him. They walked up to a member of Southern Rail who was being questioned by an officer. "Sorry constable, I need this gentleman a moment."

"Heller, what're you doing?" Markham asked.

Heller was almost panting. "Sir, you work for Southern Rail obviously?"

The Southern Rail employee's voice was hoarse and dry, only reeling from the shock of the murder. "Y... Yes. I came here after I got a call from you lot, the staff close everything at the station after 11 really."

"The last train that left this station was bound for Brighton. Does it stop anywhere?"

"The 11:55?"

"Yes!"

"Right! Erm, it stopped at Angmering at 12:25AM. So by now it must be at Goring-by-Sea or Durrington station."

Heller shook the employee's hand. "Thank you sir!" He then turned to Cowper. "Get British Transport Police to West Worthing station and Worthing station, now!"

Cowper nodded and left the scene, taking out his radio.

"The net is closing in on our Mr. Stevens it seems." Heller announced, victoriously.

Back in Worthing, at West Worthing station, the Barnham train slowed to a halt. Only two passengers left, Jeffrey Stevens, and a woman from separate carriages. Stevens looked as if he had seen a ghost, as he quickly overtook the large woman, and bolted straight for the open gate, leading onto Tarring Road opposite a pub. In the quiet of the night, Stevens hurried over the level crossings towards the long stretch of road called Becket Road, an easy route to Worthing station via Pavilion Road. As he passed into the neighbourhood, the distant wailing of a police siren filled the quiet of the night. A British Transport Police patrol car, flashing quickly than the rate of human blinking, sped up Tarring Road, screeching and stopped dead in front of West Worthing station. Three officers got out and headed through the open gate, not knowing that they had just narrowly missed Stevens.

Several minutes after, Mark Hobbes had already left his home. He was making his way up Chesswood Road, which was filled with the harsh and bullying breeze of the windy night, rusting all the bushes and trees, which only added to Hobbes' fear. His target was Homefield Park, which he passed into after watching his back. Homefield Park was totally empty, and was a large park in the centre of Worthing. Hobbes took out the flash from his phone and followed the pathway, which eventually felt like a spiral pathway. Hobbes was feeling queasy and dizzy, but stopped when he heard footsteps in the leaves lurk behind him. He stopped, and froze. After breaking free from his freeze frame, he slowly turned. To his worst fear, he saw a hooded figure standing in the entrance of the park, hands in kangaroo pockets. The figure was waiting expectantly. Hobbes gulped, hands trembling. It took Hobbes some time to make it to the hooded figure. The figure then held out his hand, a silent order for Hobbes to stop. The killer was wearing a black mask underneath the hoodie, so it almost looked like there was nothing beyond the hoodie. Hobbes was sweating and nearly in tears, for the killer approached him imposingly. The killer held out his hand. Hobbes took out from his coat pocket, a clump of hair. The killer viciously took it, and then indicated with his pointy and scrawny thumb for Hobbes to leave the park via the entrance. Hobbes nodded, and without a word, obeyed and ran out of the park. The killer simply stood in the shadows of the park, waiting.

By 1:00AM, the body was being examined by a second doctor at Barnham station. A letter, placed neatly in the tracks, was picked up by an officer.
"James, do you think it was Stevens?" Cowper handed Heller a cup of coffee, as they stood on the platform watching the doctors, forensics and officers.
"I never guess my friend." Heller took the cup. "We'll find out. After all the framing of people recently, I've learnt that if you fixate on one certain suspect, then you'll end up thinking it *is* them. We'll find out eventually." Heller then took a sip of his coffee.

Knight crept up, looking spooked, to Heller. "Sir…"
"Yes?"
"There's… There's been another murder."
Heller and Cowper immediately threw their heads at each other, looking discomposed.
"In Worthing, Homefield Park." Knight added.
"Why didn't those officers catch Stevens at the station!?" Cowper hissed.
"Gregory, remember what I said… Right, thank you Knight. Get some transportation ready for us."
Knight disquietly crept away.
"Murdering cunt…!" Heller threw his cup of coffee to the ground.
"James… I… I really don't think that we'll get him…"
"Don't say that mate."
"But look! For fuck sake, *two* murders in the space of an hour! He's insulting us, he's cleverer than us and is taunting us about it! I just, I really don't think we're gonna be able to do it."
Heller took Cowper gently aside.
"Listen here Greg, these four women have been humiliated, cut up as if they mean nothing! I don't need to eloquently describe how brutal and callous these slayings are, but we *will* do these fallen women justice, and we *will* find the killer. And trust me, it had better be you who finds him, because if I do, I'll kill him."
Cowper glanced, perturbed by this, at his colleague.
"Trust me, I'll fucking have him."
Heller then stormed off, stuffing his hands in his pockets, determined in his mind for blood. The killer would die at the hands of his own knife, and as far as James Heller was concerned, he was going to be the one to do it.

Chapter Eight
Vanishing Act

The patrol car, driven by Knight, had been silent for most of the journey. Cowper watched the passing motorways for the duration. Heller was reading the letter on a loop.
"These letters are obviously written before hand, we all know that." Heller was trying to break the silence. Cowper nodded.
"What does the letter say?" Knight asked.
Heller ready out the crumpled letter, attached with a Polaroid of Lewis, close up, on the tracks:

```
"Dear Detective Inspector James
Heller,
```

```
I guess I'm back on track now,
Halloween, the special night. I'm
gonna stain it, forever. Nobody will
forget this particular night. But, I'm
gonna confess one thing to you. This
one really gave me the feels, the
adrenaline... Making fucking mincemeat
of my fourth victim, at a bloody train
station. I mean it looked empty, but
there were two other people there.
Slaughtering her, cutting her up,
whilst the unknowing commuters were on
the other side of the station. Jesus,
it felt incredible.

I'm not finished just yet,
The Midnight Murderer."
```

"Maybe if we got that letter sooner, then we could have stopped the next killing…" Cowper suggested.

"No. There's no way that could happen, even with all our manpower searching throughout Worthing, he would just hide. It's all a game to him."

Cowper was checking his phone, when on Facebook, the Sussex Police page identified the fourth victim. "You two, the Barnham victim's been identified. 21-year-old Megan Lewis of Brighton."

The car went back to complete silence, right until it reached the outside of Homefield Park. It was approaching half one in the morning, Worthing slept unknowing and unworried. Heller and Cowper presented their warrant cards to two officers on the entrance, before entering the grim park. It was filled with the usual murder investigation team, but for the two men, they couldn't see a body.

"Well, where is it?" Cowper was even looking around him.

"You're looking in the wrong direction." Heller noted, looking up to the sky. Cowper joined his direction, to which he covered his mouth and gagged in pure horror. Hanging from a tree, overlooking the children's playground of the park, was the naked and literally gutted body of the fifth victim of the Midnight Murderer. She was swinging gently in the breeze from a strong rope. Her insides were slipping out from her abdomen, with most of her intestines sprawled on the grass below her, floating in a puddle of dark red blood. The nose had been cut off, left on the ground, with her face savagely made a total mess of. Her breasts were also sliced off, with a small gash on the throat by the knife, enough so that the rope could be embedded inside the wound. Lastly, the heart was cut in half in the grass.

"Fucking hell…" Cowper gagged once again.

"Now you understand why I'm gonna have the Midnight Murderer. I'm giving him a fucking death sentence." Heller walked over closer to the scene, composing himself. "I'd be surprised if we identify her at this rate."

Cowper took interest in her hand. "Hey, look at her hand. She's got her fist clenched. She must be holding something."

Heller pondered the suggestion, before turning to the officers beside him. "Has she been photographed?"

"Yes sir."
"Good, then get her down from there. She's got hold of something. But be careful, some of her insides might… You know…"
The officers nodded as one radioed for a ladder.
"Speaking of a ladder, the killer presumably used a ladder, we'll have to search for one nearby." Heller lit his cigarette.
"James, not here, it's a crime scene…"
"I'll do what I bloody well want. We need that body down, now."
Within minutes, officers had carefully carried the body down from a ladder. The body had been hanging about 20 feet up. Surprisingly, none of her insides fell out. The two officers immediately placed the body onto a stretcher, where an ambulance crew was waiting. Heller ran over to the body, putting on his gloves. Cowper joined him.
"Let's see what she's holding." Heller turned her fist and opened it up from the vice grip. In her palm, was a large clump of hair. Heller put it in the evidence bag. "See if it matches anyone who has tried to join the force before."
"Sir?"
"Because, Cowper, you remember joining as a police constable all those years ago, you get strands of your hair removed don't you? It's a possibility that the killer also has a hatred of the police."
Cowper nodded as he took the evidence bag.
"Get her to the mortuary, I'll join you." Heller ordered the ambulance crew. "I'll catch him for you, I promise." Heller whispered in the ear of the victim, before she was removed and taken to the ambulance. Heller smiled

tastelessly at Cowper, before the ambulance doors were closed and it went on its way.

At daybreak, Cowper was reading through papers, once again, in the common room. He hadn't taken off his coat yet. Heller then entered.
"Stubbs identified her, she is 32-year-old Rachel Harris of Ferring. She was leaving a party around midnight in Lancing."
"That's quite a walk?"
"Her phone died. She must have reached Chesswood Road, where the killer walks up to her, perhaps talks to her. Then, she turns, maybe he tells her he'll walk her home, when he smashes her face against that stone wall. Knocks her out cold, then he kills her and hangs her from the tree." Heller decided as he took another look at the chalk board of the common room, which was filled.
"We found the ladder, by the way."
"Good good, and what about that hair?"
Cowper said nothing. Instead, he handed Heller the papers he had been reading. Heller took a moment to skim-read it.
"The hair follicles match those belonging to Mark Hobbes…" Heller looked up at Cowper. "Anything else?"
"He became a PCSO in 2015, left after six months. They are a definite match."
"Right, well, we'll have to get a warrant to arrest him." Heller put the papers on a clean desk.
"How long will it take?"

"With *this* evidence, shouldn't take too long. I think Green has recalled the surveillance teams on us."
"Good, I guess we can go and find him?"
"Until we get the warrant, yes. Oh, did you hear back from the Commissioner?"
The two men began to leave the common room.
"Unsurprisingly, no."

Back at Hobbes' flat, he urgently paced up and down in a jumpy way. Stevens watched him calmly.
"I just don't see how you can be so fucking calm about all this!"
"I'm trying to remain calm, working myself up will only make things worse…" Stevens did have a hint of skittishness in his voice.
"Anyway, what did he say?"
"I'm to… To hand myself in, tell then exactly what's happened, and that I pretty much clubbed that girl at Barnham. But now I've been released from the blackmail."
Hobbes got closer to Stevens. "And… What about me?"
Stevens opened his mouth to speak, but no words came out.
"Jeffrey!"
"You've got one last task to do… But you must go on the run, hide out in Shoreham or Lancing for a bit, until November the 4th."
"Why November the 4th?"
"On that day, you've gotta… Gotta go to the Shoreham Cement Factory."

Hobbes shook his head. Full of anxiety, he sat down and let his head collapse into his hands. Stevens looked highly concerned.

"He's not gonna contact us any longer though, so I'm telling you what he told me."

Stevens then joined Hobbes, sitting next to him. He was about to put his hand comfortingly on Hobbes' shoulder, but stopped himself.

"What am I meant to do when I get there?" Hobbes mumbled, his head still in his hands.

"There's... Fucking hell, I dunno where to start!"

"Just bloody tell me!"

Stevens quickly grabbed a half full can of beer and gulped huge amounts of it.

"When you've quite finished drowning your fucking sorrows..."

"Sorry." Stevens put the now empty can on the table, next to the pile of four that Hobbes had left. "There'll be a briefcase waiting there. Inside, is a... A bomb."

Hobbes immediately straightened upright. "A bomb?"

"You've gotta take the bomb. It'll already be set with a time of five minutes. The next day, November the 5th, you've gotta call the police station in the morning. Once you have done that, tell them you'll speak to Detective Inspector James Heller. Tell him, you'll meet him at the Costa at Tesco in Durrington, alone. Once he's there, you'll have to... To leave the bomb with him."

Hobbes froze. "What...?"

"You've got to leave the bomb with Heller, make an excuse to leave for a few minutes."

"So, I'm an assassin!? Killing the fucking lead detective!"

"But then you are free mate, totally free!"
Hobbes was shaking once again, fixated on staring at the floor.
"Here's forty quid, get a train to Shoreham-by-Sea, survive off of the money till the 4th. I'm sorry, but... I've got to go." Stevens put two twenty-pound notes in Hobbes' hands and hastily left the living room. Hobbes was left with the impending thought that he may have to kill Detective Inspector James Heller.

Stevens sat waiting in the interview room, once again, in a calm attitude. Heller had already began questioning him.
"So, Jeffrey, can you explain what's been going on?"
Stevens sighed. "It's a long story."
"I've got plenty of time."
Stevens scratched his face. "So, around October 20... Something, I started getting texted by a random number. This guy claimed to be the killer, and basically told me he'd frame me for the murder unless I did what he said."
Heller frowned. "What exactly did this person have on you?"
"Well, you're not gonna believe this. But he claimed he had a clump of my hair. A huge fucking clump too!"
Heller glanced at the officer next to him, who was the tired Knight. Despite being exhausted, Knight too shared the seriousness of the allegation that Heller did.
"He said he'd plant it on the body of Abby Luther, you know, the seafront victim."
"So, by making his allegation, Mr. Stevens, you are admitting to knowing the killer?"

Stevens hesitantly nodded.

"How so?"

"Well, it should like be on record or something, but back in June, me and this bloke at the pub got into a fight. I mean we were both drunk, don't remember what it was about. But he pulled a large amount of my hair out, I remember well, because it hurt more than the bloody hangover the next day."

Heller was violently writing notes down. "Who is this man?"

"Well check on your police records."

"I want to hear it from *you* first."

"Harry Daines." Stevens answered immediately, almost taken aback from Heller's sudden loud voice. It was a few moments before the silence of the interview room was broken.

"So, explain the events of Tuesday the 31st October Mr. Stevens." Heller was still taking notes.

"I met up with Mark Hobbes, Victoria Park, around 8 or 8:30. I told him what the killer had texted me. Mark was meant to hand over a clump of his *own* hair to the killer at a designated location after midnight, whereas before midnight, I was meant to have got to Barnham." Stevens took a few moments to compose himself. "I went from West Worthing to Barnham, where I saw this young woman. She was drunk, heavily. Under the killer's instructions, I had to basically render her unconscious, and leave her on the tracks for the killer. So, that's… That's what I did."

Heller leant back in the chair. "So, you may as well have been the man behind the knife?"

"No!" Stevens snapped like a twig. "I was fearing for my life, that I'd turn into Hobbes! Become a depressed, mentally unstable alcoholic! Besides, like I said to him, for all I know, *he* could be the Midnight Murderer. Of course I regret what I did last night, and I know I'm never gonna be able to get it out of my life, but I just wanted to be freed. You lot would have me done for as the killer had he planted my hair!"

The rant raised the eyebrows of both officers in the room, almost as if they were impressed.

"So, you believe Mark Hobbes or Harry Daines, is the Midnight Murderer?" Knight asked.

Stevens nodded.

"But which one?" Heller leant back forward.

Stevens did not say a word.

In the hallway at a coffee machine, Knight returned to a waiting Heller with some files. He slammed them into Heller's chest.

"27th of June 2018. Jeffrey Robert Stevens and Harry Daines both got into a fight outside the Swallows Return, where the significant injuries detailed were that Stevens broke Daines' nose and hand."

"What else?"

"And Daines pulled out a large clump of Stevens' hair…" Knight's voice added in interest. "It was enough to leave an obvious smaller patch of hair. Both men were booked for drunk and disorderly conduct and GBH, but both decided to drop charges the following day."

Heller slurped some more coffee. "They had their fingerprints taken, obviously?"

"Yep. But the killer hasn't yet left a single print."
"I know, but here's our new suspect constable." Heller announced as he took out a mugshot photo from the files of Harry Daines. A young and small man with the equivalent to teenage fluff for facial hair on his face, Daines had an arched expression on his smooth skinned face, almost giving off the feeling of pure evil.
"One thing though." Knight began.
"I know what your gonna say. Stevens deleted at least two texts from the killer."
"So, how do we know that he's telling the truth about the killer threatening him with the clump of hair in the second text?"
"We can't. We *could* believe what he says about deleting them, thinking it was a prank… Texter?" Heller broke off. "But anyway, I've just found something by looking at the documents…"
"Oh, and what's that?"
"Knight, tell me what the killer's number is?"
"Right! Erm… 07476532244."
Heller then gave Knight one of the papers from the file.
"And what's Harry Daines' number?"
Knight's face dropped. Harry Daines mobile number, in the files, was listed as 07476532244.

Chapter Nine
Vanishing Act

"What do you mean he's gone?" Heller was angry, arms crossed and unmoving, he simply looked down upon Cowper.

"Whoa, don't start taking your man period out on me James! I said he's gone, Mark Hobbes has gone. His flat is empty, not leaving any clues whatsoever."

"Fucksake!" Heller spun round, back facing Cowper. "We'll have to mount out a search for him. We'll get the news to flash his photo up, see if anything turns up."

"I'll see to it soon, but more importantly, you say there's a new suspect?"

"Harry Daines, his number is a match to the killer's number."

"If it *is* the killer's number…"

"Come on man, it is for certain. Also, you know about the fight between Stevens and Daines?"

Cowper sat down. "And the clump of hair? Yep."

Heller sat down in his desk chair, opposite Cowper. "So, we've gotta find him and bring him in for questioning."

"I did a bit of Facebook stalking…"

"Well… We're all guilty of that, but I don't wanna know about your single man habits."

"No, you don't understand. I stalked Harry Daines, he's leaving for Spain later tonight, at Gatwick."

"When?"

"Well, he said in a post he's planning on getting there around 9:00PM."

Heller loosened his already lose tie. "Well, he's gonna be going on a little detour then. Can you get ready to release Stevens?"

"Is that wise? Very soon."

"I've questioned everything that I possibly can on him. He is oddly calm about it, I will admit. But there's nothing on him, and Daines looks guiltier of it right now."

There was a knock on the office door. Standing there, was Markham, with a distressed looking Emerson.

"Get that fucking wank stain out of my office Markham." Heller ordered as he took out his newspaper to begin reading.

"I must speak to you immediately Detective!" Emerson entered the office, standing right next to Heller, who was less than pleased.

"What the fuck do you want? Eh?"

Emerson looked around him, helping himself to a chair.

"What is it Emerson?" Cowper rolled his eyes.
"You know I'm not the killer, right?"
"We do." Heller wasn't taking any interest.
"Good, then can you please tell the public out there? They are hell bent on making my life a misery!"
"What do you mean? You should be held on remand!"
"Bail."
Heller threw his paper on the floor. "Fucking bail?! When there's evidence? Fucking ridiculous."
"Listen! At my flat, they've painted 'the Midnight Murderer' on my door. I get attacked, every day, more than once." Emerson then took off his cap to reveal a bloody gash on his balding head. "I got bottled last night when they burst in."
Heller got up and picked Emerson up by his sleeve. "Then in future, *call* the police instead of making yourself comfy in my office." Heller dragged Emerson to the door, where Markham was waiting. "If it makes you feel any better, I will come round tomorrow morning, tell your neighbours what *really* happened that night to Abby Luther."
Emerson shook his head for an answer.
"The sexual assault! The high ups decided to not fucking tell people about it, but I will. Then that'll clear your name as the fucking Midnight bloody Murderer, now get out you piece of shitty filth!" Heller shoved Emerson out into the hallway, before slamming the door shut.

Later, in the evening, the pissed off looking Harry Daines was now sitting in the interview room. Heller and Markham were taking charge of the questioning.

"So, your claiming that your phone was stolen around July/August time?"
"Yeah." Daines was a very blunt individual.
"By who?"
"Dunno. When you leave it in your pocket, turn your back, and it's gone innit?"
"Particularly in a pub, am I right?"
"Yeah. Look, I ain't gonna like get all pissy with you, because I know deep down that I ain't no killer."
"Thank you for that." Heller instantly moved on. "So, have you got a new phone?"
"Nah."
"Really? A 24-year-old man in 2018 doesn't have a phone?"
"I told you! Nah, I don't, alright?"
"You see I don't believe you."
Daines protruded his bitter dry lips. "Don't you?"
"No. So perhaps you could tell us where it is?"
"Nah, 'cause I don't have it." Daines still had his arms crossed, he said back calmed and laid back since the start of the interview.
"Don't bullshit us Harry! Where have you hidden the phone?"
"Nowhere, it was stolen, I told you this! You thick or something?"
"I must be if you think I'm gonna believe your story. Where is the phone?"
"I dunno!"
Heller sighed like a parent trying to calm down a toddler.
"Don't huff and puff at me."
"Or what? You'll kill me?"

Daines threw the chair back, slamming the wall, as he got straight up and growled at Heller. "Don't you fucking dare!"

Markham got up, ready to defend Heller.

"Sit back down! I'm not finished." Heller said casually.

Daines defeatedly sat back down.

"Now, we know you have an angry streak, we just witnessed it. But also, you know why Jeffrey Stevens started on you, back then, don't you?"

Daines was biting his nails like they were chewy meat.

"Yes, but I'm not proud of it yeah?"

"Can you tell us what it was?"

"I... I touched up this woman, in the pub. I was drunk for fuck sake, not that I'm defending it though. Suppose that makes me look guiltier."

Heller nodded. "Yes. Interview terminated at 22:42PM." Heller stopped the recording.

The next day, Heller felt very little difference in his struggles with the case.

"So, you've caught the Midnight Murderer at last have you?" Green smiled in total joy.

"Maybe." Heller remarked, looking outside from the window of his office.

"What do you mean maybe? The phone numbers match, he got Jeffrey Stevens' hair months ago. It all adds up James!"

"Yeah, okay, so our so far clever killer gets caught over something like this? Sir, he'd cover his tracks, wouldn't let himself get caught this easily."

"Hey, *you* were the one who charged him if I remember rightly…" Green indicated accusingly.

"Yes, yes. With what you just said, the public may think we have got the Midnight Murderer. I want them to have some hope to latch onto, not constantly live in fear. But I believe the killer is still out there, he's got to be."

Green, of course, would never agree with Heller. "I'm sure you'll do your best efforts to locate the phone. Who knows, maybe even the hair?" Green then laughed.

"It's not a laughing matter Charles!"

Green's face fell. He placed his cup of tea onto the desk, attempting to keep his cool.

"Oh, what's the matter? Did I not call you 'sir'?" Heller mocked in a crying voice.

"You have one last chance after the antics that you pulled the other night."

"Without that, Stevens wouldn't have been questioned, and so Daines wouldn't be in custody. We'd be as clueless as we were at the fucking start!"

Green, in a twist of events, simply picked his cup of tea up and remained calm. "Maybe Mark Hobbes has the answers."

"Yes, well, we found CCTV footage of him at Shoreham station. Have no idea where he went beyond there."

"I'm sure you'll do your best." Green said, almost encouragingly, before leaving the office. As Green nodded at Cowper, Cowper then entered.

"Morning Greg." Heller smiled.

"Morning sir. Daines said he wants to speak to you."

"I will later, when we're back from paying Emerson another visit."

Cowper joked. "Looking forward to it sir?"

Heller wasn't going to dignify Cowper with a response. Then, Stubbs ran into the office.

"Long time no see stranger!" Heller was for once being polite to the journalist.

"Heller, you've got to take a look at this." Stubbs presented another envelope. Heller took the envelope and neatly opened it. He read out the contents of the letter:

```
"To the Worthing Herald,

Please do send this to the police, I
may be one clever bastard, but I don't
have the capability to kill off
another within the space of a day, so
I have no body to leave a letter with.
Is it a hoax, or isn't it?

All I'm going to say, James Heller, is
that I have one burning passion.
Remember, remember, the fifth of
November...


Lots of love,
The Midnight Murderer"
```

Cowper took the letter. Having heard Heller read it, Cowper was only interested in reading the final lines. "Now what does he mean by the 5th of November part?" Stubbs took off his glasses.

"Well, we all know that it's bonfire night." Heller's mind was blank.

Cowper felt the need to correct his partner. "Guy Falkes night."

"Bonfire night." Heller knew he was right.

"Guy Falkes night." Cowper insisted.

"Bonfire ni- Look, we've gotta focus on this damn letter, not the bloody night."

"That's it!" Stubbs snapped his finger.

Heller and Cowper turned onto Stubbs.

"Don't you see? If it isn't a hoax, then the killer is going to do something massive on Guy Falkes night."

"Yeah, yeah. I mean he may well be planning to do something on Bonfire night, or perhaps even during the day."

"Another murder..." Stubbs sighed.

"I don't think so. The use of the phrase 'burning passion'. Well he isn't exactly gonna burn the next victim, is he?"

"It's not his modus operandi." Cowper agreed with Heller. He then turned the letter, where he saw more text.

"There's more text..." He uttered.

"What does it say?" Heller demanded.

Cowper read out the words:

```
"P.S...

I'm not Mark Hobbes, Jeffrey Stevens
or Harry Daines.
```

```
I might not be Eddie Stubbs, Robert
Hall or Nathan Emerson.

It's possible that I'm not Dr. Richard
Cuthbertson, DI Nicholas Hollis or PC
Ralph Knight.

It's likely or unlikely that I'm
Sergeant John Markham, DI Greg Cowper
or DI James Heller.

But then again, I could be any of
those people."
```

"He's playing games." Cowper put the letter on the desk. Heller nodded. "Yes, but *who's* gonna win the game?"

Emerson's flat had not changed one bit, it was still a mess, but even messier than it was last time. Outside, having living on the ground floor landing, the hounding press flashed photograph after photograph, with the general public roaring at their prey. Emerson genuinely felt scared, living in fear, and rightfully so. Despite the blinds being closed, Emerson felt that they could see his every move.
"See... Whatever you think of me, I'm being hounded, and I'm living in constant fear. It's your job to do something about it." Emerson sounded desperate.

Heller shrugged his shoulders carelessly. "Not really. We've got two officers coming here, they'll get them away. Just give it time, they'll eventually go away."
Emerson got to his aching old feet. "But they won't, they won't!"
"We'll announce to them shortly that we have a suspect in custody, okay?" Cowper was also carefree and careless.
"I need bloody protective custody!"
"Yeah, well, that won't be happening Mr. Emerson." Heller then turned to Cowper. "Tell them we have a suspect in custody."
Cowper nodded obediently before leaving the flat.
"You're just doing this to spite me…" Emerson fell back into his tatty old chair.
"Yes, that and due to the fact that I'm trying to catch this killer, so why the fuck do you think I'd give a damn about your tiny little problems?"
"Trying to catch…? But you have a suspect you said." Heller ignored Emerson.
"Do your job and help me for god sake!"
Heller took out his pack of cigarettes and threw them at Emerson. "Knock yourself out. Or worse, kill yourself maybe?"
Emerson watched the smug detective leave the flat. Emerson then collapsed in a heap on the floor in complete distress.

In the small front garden of the flats, the media crowds were held back by two officers. Cowper felt slightly awkward with all the cameras being on him. Adjusting his tie, he cleared his throat.

"I can confirm to you all, that we have a 24-year-old suspect in custody. He has been arrested on suspicion of the murders of Jessica Powell, Abby Luther, Katie Brown, Megan Lewis and Rachel Harris. We will update you all on any further developments."

Cowper then nodded, very awkwardly, before he made his way to the patrol car where Heller followed. Despite the crowds pinning questions to the two detectives, the two officers held back the crowds, as Heller and Cowper got into the car which drove off.

Daines sat alone in his cell, in brown joggers and a plain brown sweater. Then, the keys were heard jangling on the other side of the cell door. Finally, the door opened, where Daines saw Heller standing with an officer. Heller nodded with a smile at him, and got into the cell, the door slamming shut behind him.

"You wanted to speak to me?" Heller sat down next to Daines, who was much calmer.

"Yes, Inspector…"

"How are you feeling? They been treating you well?"

Daines nodded.

"So, what is it?"

"I just wanted to say, to you and only you, that I really genuinely don't know where my phone is. I haven't had one since I lost that one. Come on, I ain't rich, it's not like I can even get a half decent one."

Heller nodded. "We searched your house, found nothing incriminating whatsoever. So I'm kinda starting to believe you Harry."

"Then why can't I be released?" Daines nearly sounded like he was about to choke up.

Heller sighed. "It's not that simple. The fact is, we still have the numbers matching, and this hair."

"Oh, come on. Like I'd stuff Jeffrey Stevens' hair into my pocket and keep it! Has the number been used since I was arrested?"

"It hasn't."

"Great. Even more guilty."

"I don't think you're the Midnight Murderer."

Daines seemed hopeful. "What? Really though?"

"Yeah. The Herald received a letter, same type of font, similar style of writing that the killer uses. The letter gives six names, including you, and me to be honest. It's taunting us, like all other letters. It could be a hoax, but I doubt it."

"So you're still going to hold me here?"

"You and I could hatch a good plan here Harry."

"Huh?"

Heller got closer to an interested but dumb looking Daines. "This letter mentions something possibly happening on November the 5th, that's in four day's time. Until then, if you stay here in the cell, I'll make sure you have more food and drink. If something *does* happen, I'll see to it that you are released."

Daines hesitated. "Only if like… Like the papers and stuff don't know that I've been arrested."

Heller shook his head. "They don't."

Daines held out his hand. Heller and he shook on it with smiling faces.

Heller returned to his office. He saw Knight standing there reading a paper.
"No Cowper?"
"It's his lunch break sir."
"Oh." Heller then sat down and studied the letter again.
"Hey, have you heard about this sir?"
Heller took off his glasses. "Heard about what?"
"Two local women claim that Harry Daines has sexually assaulted them in the past two weeks."
"Fucking attention seekers. How the hell do they know he's been arrested anyway?"
Knight put the paper on the desk. "Guess they saw him get arrested by you and Cowper, so they naturally presume he's the Midnight Murderer."
"Well, I'll be speaking to them very soon then."
"So, what are we doing till the 5th?"
Heller laid back in his chair. "Playing the waiting game, Knight. Playing the waiting game."

November 4th, late evening. The old cement factory in Shoreham was a castaway near the motorway, almost nowhere near Shoreham. It was your typical abandoned, mostly rusty old factory you could find anywhere in Britain. The large industrial area was totally empty, except from the small figure of Mark Hobbes outside. Using his feet to fight through the overgrown grass outside, Hobbes reached the entrance. The striking and intimidating factory made him feel tiny and insignificant, but he was now totally desperate. Everyday since he ran, he had been drunk. He just wanted his freedom, and was to make sure he'd get it. There was no door, just the door frame and the dark beyond. Hobbes took out his phone and turned on the flashlight, before swaying inside, for he was tipsy. Inside, his footsteps on the metal floor clanged and echoed throughout the vast kingdom inside the factory. Shining the flashlight, Hobbes saw several metal floors above him, all rusted and dangerous looking, with missing bolts and nails holding them in place. The walls were the colour of dark red blood, and directly in front of Hobbes were metal railings, with some patches of remaining and peeling paint. Left at the bottom of the railings, was a brown leather briefcase. Hobbes felt as if that briefcase had sobered him completely. Sniffing with a terrible cold, Hobbes picked up the briefcase. A paper note fell off, which simply indicated to Hobbes how to leave the bomb. The instructions that Stevens had told him, and those of the sheet of paper, were imprinted on his brain. For a while, Hobbes stood looking in uncertainty at the briefcase, before he strolled off out of the cement factory.

The next morning, Heller was fast asleep in his chair. The straining sun broke through the grey clouds outside, and barely broke through the blinds of the Detective's office. Markham entered with a coffee, where he slapped Heller on the face. Heller's head was knocked clean off his shoulders as he yawned.

"Sorry sir…" Markham was secretly pissing himself in laughter.

"Mmm…" Heller mumbled. He grabbed the coffee. "Three sugars?"

"Oh, no… Sorry sir. I didn't know you had sugar."

Heller handed Markham the coffee back. Markham hadn't reached the door, before the phone on the desk rung. He picked it up, way before the snail-paced Heller.

"DI Heller's office." Markham was truly smug this morning, and Heller was not in the mood for it.

Markham's face changed. He then gave Heller the phone. "The call was redirected from reception. You'll want to answer James…"

Heller kept watching Markham as he answered. "Heller here."

"Inspector… It's me, Mark Hobbes…"

Heller certainly didn't need coffee to wake up anymore. "Mark. Where are you?"

"Listen, I can't talk now. But I *will* talk to you, this morning. Just… Not over the phone, and not at the station. I'm not a killer."

"Okay. Where and when?"

"C… Costa…"

Heller was waiting for more of an answer. "Yeah… What the Costa in Scotland?"

"This… This isn't the time to be funny, I have valuable information for you about the killer. Meet me at 10:00AM at the Costa at Tesco, in Durrington. There, I shall speak to you."

Heller opened his mouth to speak, but Hobbes had hung up.

Chapter Ten
A Burning Passion

Heller was with Cowper in his office.
"This is strange, very strange…" Heller held his hands thoughtfully on his hips.
"So, he wants to meet you for a coffee and a nice cosy little chat?" Cowper was doubtful.
"Greg, this really is bloody important. He's the most important person in the investigation right now. I believe he has met the killer."
Cowper cautiously closed the door. "This is between us and Markham, right?"
"Yes. Green finds out, he'll have the entire force there to arrest Hobbes. No, no. I must talk to the guy myself."
"He might try something… Remember, today's the 5th?"

Heller did not realise this until he looked at the calendar. "It's a risk I'll have to take. If Green finds out, that could be me off the case, and I can't let that happen."
Heller got up, the clock was at 8:49AM. Cowper then grabbed his coat and handed it to him, to which Heller put it on.
"You'll have the radio with you?"
"Yes, but it'll be switched off Greg. It has to be, nothing must raise Hobbes' suspicions. This could be our last chance to get closer to the killer."
Cowper looked the most worried Heller had ever seen him. "Who knows? You may already be closer than you think."
Heller raised his eyebrows. "Maybe. I'll have my phone on me, but stay here. Just tell people that I've taken the day off, sick or something."
"Good luck James."
Heller nodded with a friendly and acknowledging smile, before putting on his gloves and scarf and leaving the common room.

Soon after, Heller parked his car in the heavily filled car park. Tesco dominantly overlooked the car park and surrounding areas, even the smaller shops such as WHSmith and Subway, that were attached to the store. Heller started recording a voice memo on his phone, before stuffing it into his pocket. Heller took a good look around him as he slowly walked across the icy ground, eager to see if he could spot Hobbes. Without seeing him, Heller entered the store. The warmth inside embraced him, and he took off the scarf. Heller stopped, where he had a good look of the area. Right at the far end, wedged away in a cosy corner, was Costa. Heller instantly saw the scruffy Hobbes sitting at a table, with two coffees. He was waiting dead on time for the Detective. Inhaling, preparing for any eventuality, Heller speed walked to Costa. Hobbes, who had his palms wrapped around his coffee mug, immediately caught sight of the approaching man. Hobbes got goose bumps spreading all over, all his hairs on his arms and legs standing on end. He grabbed the mug even tighter, his heart thumping so much that his body felt like a stirring earthquake about to start. Heller, meanwhile, felt nothing but tense. He took one emotionless nod at Hobbes, before pulling out the chair opposite and sat down.

"Thanks for the coffee, could do with it to."

Hobbes did not look up. The pair felt in their own tense world, as if anything around them was a blur.

"So, not gonna say anything are we?"

"Sorry… Erm, yes, yes. The evidence, against me, it doesn't prove that I'm the killer." Hobbes cleared his croaky throat. The briefcase was tucked away next to his foot. "My polaroid and disposable camera, they were stolen by the killer."

"There was no letter with Rachel Harris, the Homefield Park victim, and with Megan North, there was a letter but no photo."

"I started getting texts, from the killer. My number is on my photography site, as is my address. He blackmailed me, said he'd plant my polaroid and disposable camera on the bodies, to make me look guilty. You… You must understand, that made me live in constant fear!"

Heller was understanding. "I get it. So what happened? Did you hurt any of the victims, like Jeffrey Stevens?"
"No. Me and him are mates, he gave me some money to cope after running away."
"So, these drinks are on Stevens? You and he seem very close."
"We were, years ago. Now it's just more of seeing each other, sometimes, at the pub. He was also blackmailed, and told to go to you lot by the killer, so now he's free."
Heller was drinking his coffee. "And how are you going to be set free?"
Hobbes made up an excuse hastily. "Coming here. To talk to you."
"Okay, so what happened? Again, did you hurt any victims?"
"No, not at all. With the one on the seafront, I was told to wait on the other side of the shelter. So when Emerson ran, and the killer killed her underneath the pier, I had to shout out that there had been a murder."
"To make it look like Emerson did it." Heller concluded.
"Yes." Hobbes took a brief moment to drink quickly from his mug. "With the one in the park, I actually… Saw, the killer. He wore that black hoodie, black trousers, but must have been wearing a black mask. Because… There was no face, like the hood was empty. I had to hand over a clump of my own hair."
"Yes, we took a look. It matched the hair follicles taken when you trained to be a PCSO."
Hobbes nodded. "I thought that would happen."
"You must have more to discuss?"

Hobbes hesitated. "Yes… I do. You see, I drove here. There's some evidence, to show that… That I know who the killer is."

"What does driving here have to do with that?"

Hobbes finished his coffee. "My car, it has some incriminating evidence in the boot."

"So who is the killer then Hobbes?"

Hobbes pulled his chair back, about to get up. "You'll see in a minute." Hobbes then got up, picking up his briefcase. Heller didn't take much notice of it, and simply continued drinking his coffee. "The evidence I need is in my car, I'll go and get it. Gimme like, five minutes?"

Heller nodded. "But don't think about running off."

Hobbes nodded. He then put the briefcase on a table behind him and Heller, pausing. He held his shaking hands above the briefcase. Turning back behind him, Heller had begun to read a newspaper. Turning back to look at the briefcase, getting ready to hurry away, Hobbes unclipped the briefcase. As soon as he unclipped them, in the snap of a finger, the briefcase exploded with a heavy and loud, ear piercing boom. The explosion was smaller than one would think, but exploded right in Hobbes' face. Hobbes cried out a blood curdling cry as he fell back, his face enveloped in the explosion and his arms.

Within minutes, Tesco had been evacuated. Costa wasn't damaged that much, only some empty tables and chairs had seen the full force of the blast, but a choking smokescreen filled half of the store. Forensics were everywhere, with Heller standing near his table. Heller had a huge plaster on his cheek, where a piece of shrapnel had been thrown into. Having removed it himself, Heller was better very quickly. He stood looking at Hobbes. Hobbes face resembled that of all the other victims. Cowper was with him, and they were both within the presence of a disapproving Green.

"I can't believe this… You actually met up with him, without telling *anyone*!?"

Heller nodded, not phased by the bellowing voice. He then picked up a small piece of the timer and studied it.

"Hey… That's a small clock, it's at zero. There's no time essentially."

Heller nodded at Cowper's comment. "It was deliberately faulty. The killer intended to kill him."

"We was trying to kill two birds with one stone…"

Green took the piece of the timer and threw it onto the floor. "Your lucky nobody has been killed or injured!"

"Except from Hobbes?" Heller said defensively. "Of course, he was a fucking bastard for trying to kill me, but I don't blame him. He was weak, and an easy plaything of the Midnight Murderer."

Heller left Costa and stood near some tills. Cowper and Green remained behind him. "Now, the killer is finished with his blackmailing game."

"So he's back on his own. I take it he's just gonna kill and kill, without this web of blackmail?"

"Most probably." Heller then took out a letter. "I found this in Hobbes' coat. One side gives him fake instructions about the briefcase bomb, but the rest is another letter from the killer. Hobbes must have

presumed it was a draft or was meant to give it to the station after the bomb went off."
Green snatched the letter and read it:

```
"To Sussex Police,

I'm so sorry to have capped off one of
your own, but it does make this rather
exciting doesn't it?

Now, I shall take a break. Have myself
a little holiday. When will I start
killing again? Who knows! Maybe an
early Christmas present might be an
idea?


Sorry for your loss,
The Midnight Murderer"
```

"Then you are wrong Heller! He isn't going to keep on killing." Green was simply furious with Heller.
"Not yet, no."
"I want to see you, tomorrow night at the station. I want you there too Cowper, we need to have a talk." Green put the letter in his pocket. Without a word, he walked away and left the two men.
"I'm gonna take the rest of the day off, and tomorrow." Heller cracked his knuckles. "I do get too attached to my work, a day off would help."

Cowper patted his friend on the shoulder. "I'll hold the fort then."
"Well, standing in for me if your forte…" Heller winked at Cowper.
"What do you think he's going to talk to us about?" Heller's face dropped. "I have an idea… I just hope it isn't what I'm thinking. I just hope…" Heller wandered off, in his own trail of words, before he kept his head down. He then brushed past Cowper and left him.

The evening of November 6th was not a pleasant one. Typical British weather for the winter, the rain was drumming down, the lightening flashing here and there and the thunder rumbling away. Heller parked outside the station and quickly got into the reception, darting away to try and avoid the rain. As soon as he got inside, he felt an atmosphere of forlorn. The sergeant on reception even gave Heller a smile, even though it felt forced. The entire station was silent.
"Sergeant, what's going on? Fells fucking weird around here." Heller noted that there were no voices, no telephones ringing, not even footsteps in the corridors.
"Superintendent Green is waiting in the common room for you sir, along with the Commissioner."
"At last, she's shown her face." Heller joked as he left the reception.

Waiting in the mournful common room was Green, the Commissioner and Cowper. Cowper had his coat on, as if about to leave. Green was shunned to the corner of the

room almost, as he hadn't said a word. Commissioner Grace Robins was a small and slim but had a powerful feel around her. She had a slightly fiendish and smug face and attitude, which gave her an influence over the surroundings. She was quite pretty looking, but not a pretty character. Cowper looked as if he was biting his tongue. The door was thrown open as Heller got inside.
"Commissioner Robins." He addressed with politeness.
"Inspector." The stern voice replied. "You've been called here, both you and Cowper, over a matter of great urgency."
"I'm all ears." Heller stood beside Cowper.
"Superintendent Green has already made me fully aware of your activities with Detective Inspector Gregory Cowper, Sergeant John Markham and Police Constable Ralph Knight, concerning Mark Hobbes."
Heller nodded. "We carried out our own surveillance operation."
"Yes, *without* authority from Superintendent Green, or myself. Yet when you were warned about it, you continued, on the night of October 31st."
"I see what you mean mam, but with all due respect, it allowed us to find out that Jeffrey Stevens was involved in the murders."
"You had no right Inspector! I and Green agreed to give you one last chance, you are one of the best we have. But that doesn't mean you can waltz around freely, doing whatever you want. It's not a good example to any other officer on the force."
"This shouldn't concern Greg. Please can you let him go?"

The Commissioner shook her head. "He has told us, very defiantly if I may add, that he supported these ideas. He also informed us that he supported the idea of you meeting Mark Hobbes yesterday, alone."

Heller had nothing to say.

"You are running a mockery around here James! I put you on this case because I presumed you'd simply do your job, and as you have done in the past, go above and beyond to solve this crime. But that doesn't mean going beyond the boundaries that every officer has. You had two chances, and you blew them."

Heller fully understood what was about to happen, and kept his head drawn to the floor like a sulking child.

"Detective Inspector James Heller, I regret to inform you that due to your recent actions, I am formally discharging you from this investigation, along with your partner Detective Inspector Gregory Cowper. You will be replaced by a new team of detectives, and shall not concern yourself with the case anymore. Is that understood?"

Heller lifelessly nodded.

Chapter Eleven
Judge, Jury and Executioner

After recording the entire long story, Stubbs sat back with a mug of warm coffee. Sitting opposite him, were Heller and Cowper. They wore their usual suits, due to the interview having been recorded. It had been three whole hours of them being interviewed by Stubbs, and all three were quite tired.

"Jesus. That is one hell of a story, I don't think there's ever been a serial killer case quite like this one." Stubbs sat back in his chair, with his camera still rolling on the tripod. The men sat in Cowper's living room, with the fire crackling contently in the background. The living room was quite darkened, however.

"We're approaching the end of the interview, but I've still got some questions for you two."

"Fire ahead." Cowper smiled.

"What exactly happened after you two were dismissed?"

Heller yawned. "Well, the next day, we found out that DI Leon Colbert was now in charge of the case, and what little work he and his 'team' have done so far… Me and Cowper decided to work on the case, in our own way."

"How so?"

Cowper stirred his tea. "I got James, eventually, to move in temporarily. I thought it would be easier if we worked on it from here."

"Something wrong with your place James?" Stubbs joked.

"Nah, not at all. I just didn't suggest going to mine. I keep my private life private, even from myself."

Stubbs nodded in silence.

"We got some help from Sergeant Markham, until the end of November. He was giving us the latest information, but was found out and dismissed from the case too." Cowper explained.

"Do you both have a current suspect?"

Cowper smiled and turned to Heller.

"I guess I'll explain then." Heller got comfortable in his chair. "So, definitely not Mark Hobbes. Also, not Nathan

Emerson. As we all know, he threw himself off Teville Gate at the end of November."

Heller went mute.

"So… Who do you think it is?" Stubbs was really encouraging Heller and Cowper for a definite answer.

"I said to Greg, in the early days of the investigation, that you should never fixate on one certain suspect, because once you do that, your mind tells you that *they* are the killer no matter what. But to be honest, my mind is blank. I have no idea."

"Hmm. Greg, you think the same?"

"Well Eddie…" Cowper began, but was interrupted by a knock of the door. "Excuse me." Cowper then got up and left the living room.

"James?"

"Yes?"

"One final question for you. Do you think they'll ever catch the Midnight Murderer?"

Heller thought very hard about the question. "They won't. But I will."

Stubbs and Heller smiled, but Cowper entered, and was not. He was holding an envelope. Immediately, both Heller and Stubbs were drained of the smiles, and all attention was locked onto the envelope. Cowper gave it to Heller, who ravened it open.

"What does it say?" Stubbs stopped recording on the camera.

Heller read the letter:

"`To James, Gregory and Edward,`

So, I've had my long winter break. Tonight's the night, December 31st. After writing this and posting it, it is exactly three hours until January 1st, 2019. To be honest, I have missed the infamous James Heller and his partner, Greg Cowper, working their asses off on the case. That new detective is as shit as the blocked bog.

Tonight shall be a very grave matter indeed, think I'll make it my greatest piece of artwork yet. Cannot wait to start the New Year with a bang!

**Good luck to you,
The Midnight Murderer"**

Heller had snapped right back into his sharp minded self.
"How did he know we're here?" He asked Cowper.
"That... That might be my fault. I put a post on Facebook earlier, about coming here tonight for the interview. He must have seen it."
"Eddie Stubbs, you are a genius!" Heller then kissed a confused Stubbs on his wrinkled forehead.
"That means he's friends with the killer on Facebook!" Cowper realised.
"Who are you friends with, that's been involved in the case?"

Stubbs was scanning his memory. "Let me see… Well, Harry Daines, Jeffrey Stevens, Robert Hall… Oh who else?"

"Think man, think!" Cowper was beginning to get impatient.

"Oh, yes! I'm also friends with Hobbes and… Well, that's it."

Cowper turned to Heller. "It must be Daines, it's got to be."

"You may well be right… Right now, it's either Daines, Stevens, Dr. Cuthbertson, DI Colbert or someone we haven't even considered yet." Heller was beginning to put his coat on.

"Hang on… A doctor and a Detective who has worked on the case?"

"Gotta consider anyone and everyone Eddie. The doctor, we all remember why I briefly suspected him. Colbert was only too eager to work on the case, maybe to cover his tracks."

Cowper put his coat on too.

"But… But where are you going?" Stubbs was like a small confused child surrounded by adults.

"To the station, we've got to plan getting the Midnight Murderer." Heller then quickly put his gloves on.

"But you don't even know where he'll strike!"

Heller showed Stubbs and Cowper the letter. "Look at that… "Tonight shall be a very grave matter indeed" … Don't you see? He always uses puns. Grave! He's going to strike in a graveyard, he's leaving it that clearly because he honestly believes we're that thick not to notice that. He's cocky, and that'll be his downfall."

Cowper and Stubbs had now got their coats on.

"Trust me gentlemen, we're gonna catch the Midnight Murderer. The Midnight Murders stop. Tonight!"

It seemed odd, to Knight, to see Colbert in the common room, let alone Heller's office, taking charge of the investigation. Colbert started off bright and enthusiastic to quickly solve the case, but now like everyone who had worked on the case, Colbert sat at a desk with his head in his hands. His life was being constantly drained. Sporting a thick black moustache, Colbert was quite good looking with a messy quiff, but would annoy the hell out of anyone. The room was usually quiet ever since Heller and Cowper were removed from the case. It didn't feel quite right without them.
"Alright… Go Constable, enjoy the New Year with your friends." Colbert was nearly falling asleep.
"Thank you, sir. See you next year sir." Knight headed for the door.
"Hah hah. Very funny." Colbert sat back in the chair, not knowing what to do with himself. Knight then opened the door, where to his surprise and joy, Heller and Cowper were standing.
"James!"
"Ralph." Heller muttered, as he entered the common room. "DI Colbert?"
Colbert rose up. "Here! You two have been booted off the case. It's mine now!" Colbert felt defensive.
"Yes, and what a fine mess you've made of it already." Heller remarked.
"I'm getting you out of here…" Colbert reached for the telephone, but his hand was clamped down on by Heller.

Heller then put the letter on the desk in front of the stunned Colbert. "What is the meaning of this?"

"Once you read that, you won't be calling reception." Heller let go, and allowed Colbert to read the letter. Stubbs and Cowper stood with Knight, waiting.

"Good god… How did you get this?"

"It was posted through Cowper's door about twenty minutes ago, whilst we were doing an interview. Now, you've studied all the letters, right?"

"I have, yes. He does like to use his puns doesn't he?"

Heller snapped his finger. "Exactly. Now me, Greg and Eddie here, we all agree that he has a pun in that letter."

Colbert couldn't find it. "Where?"

"Where he mentions tonight being a grave matter. I believe, he is gonna kill in a graveyard." Heller opened the door to his office and threw Colbert's coat off of the chair back to Colbert, who caught it.

"Would he really leave such a big clue?" Colbert threw his coat to Knight, who caught it with rolling eyes.

"Yes. Because of everything that's happened, making Hobbes his fifth victim in the way that he did, blackmailing people… He think's he can do anything."

Colbert understood the gravity of the situation. "Well, I'll get onto Green."

"No." Cowper stood forward. "We started out on this case. We're gonna finish it."

"Are you suggesting that we all work together?" Colbert wasn't too sure.

"Yes. All of us in here, including Stubbs. The more officers we alert, the bigger the risk is of Green finding out about this before we execute the plan." Cowper explained.

"I'll call Markham, get him here. Because we all have the same passion to capture the killer. Do you know a few officers who you could trust not to tell Green?"
Colbert scratched his aching neck. "About… Three of four."
"Good good, then get them here quickly. Once we're all here, I can hatch out the plan to you all."

Shortly, the room was filled. Heller stood at the chalkboard, whilst everyone else sat down. Cowper, Stubbs, Knight, Markham, Colbert and four uniformed officers were listening totally engrossed and intently to Heller.
"Now then. We *know* that the killer is planning on striking in a graveyard. He mentions starting the new year with a bang, so my guess is that this time, he will strike *exactly* on midnight. The first four murders were committed either just before or just after midnight, with Harris being killed at around 2:00AM. Hobbes, of course, was killed in broad daylight. So, all the local graveyards in Worthing will be our priorities. Myself and Cowper shall be going to the graveyard at St Mary's Parish in Broadwater. It's a small graveyard, but not overlooked by any houses. Knight and Stubbs, you'll both be going to the other graveyard in Broadwater, Broadwater Cemetery. Colbert and Markham, you two will be going to Durrington Cemetery. Officers Phillips and Taylor, you'll be heading to Christ Church in the town centre. Officers Tomas and Jones, you two will be at St Mary's Church in Goring-by-Sea. And finally,

officers Godfrey and Burns, you'll be heading to St. Andrew's Church in Ferring."

Everyone was taking their final notes. Heller waiting until everyone had stopped.

"Okay, all understand everything?"

"Yes." Everyone barked in agreement. Everyone was excited and apprehensive to catch the Midnight Murderer.

Heller nodded proudly. "Tonight's the night we get the fucking bastard. Right, now everyone, get to your churches and graveyards."

The four officers then left, followed by Colbert, Stubbs, Knight and Markham. Heller and Cowper remained behind.

"Do you really think we'll get him tonight?" Cowper whispered.

"Of course we will. But if it's us who finds him, I'm sticking to that promise I made a while back." Heller whispered back, before leaving with Cowper. The team was ready to catch the killer.

The small graveyard of St. Mary's in Broadwater was enveloped in ominous fog. The uneven graves gave Heller and Cowper somewhere to hide, as they crouched behind a small group of them. They had been there for nearly three hours, and were actually getting bored. They still remained alert. They were in a dark corner of the graveyard, and had a slightly clear view of the rusted gate at the entrance. The streets of Broadwater, which was still in the heart of Worthing, were empty. Everyone was out at the fireworks on the seafront.

"11:50…" Cowper announced as he took a glance at his watch.

"In ten minutes, we'll have him Greg." Heller promised. His eyes were unblinking and drawn to the gate, which went to and fro gently in the wind. Another silent minute passed.

"James, I need to tell you something…" Cowper turned his back, trying to relax slightly, from the gate.

"Sure man."

"This case. It's the first biggie I've worked on. The only others I've worked on, were missing persons really. I wasn't prepared for a murder case. I can honestly say, that I'm glad I have you leading the case."

Heller was touched, but at first tried to hide it. "Bit gay that, isn't it?"

"I'm serious. We make a good team you and me."

Heller took his attention onto Cowper. "Well, I hope we investigate many more cases together."

The men smiled at each other, before they both drew their attention back to the gate. Minute after minute passed. Cowper was beginning to get worried that the killer hadn't chosen St. Mary's as the location. It was only five minutes to midnight. They were not about to give up. However, as luck would have it, two figures began to walk past the stone wall of the church. A hooded figure, all in black, grasped onto the gate.

"Here he is…" Cowper whispered. Heller indicated for him to hush with his hand gestures. The gate creaked open, and the hooded figure held his arm out politely. Appearing into view was a drunk brunette, who was laughing and giggling away.

"Why thank you…" she took her heels off and practically waltzed into the graveyard. The hooded figure closed the gate. Heller and Cowper couldn't believe that they were now eying up the Midnight Murderer, finally, after all this time. One wrong action, and he could slip through their fingers one final time.
"Oooohhhh, spooky. Why've you taken us here… Hoody…" the woman began to slur her words. The killer was mute and said nothing. "I see, gone all silent, have we? Silent treatment…" the woman then grabbed the strings of the killer's hoodie and pulled them enticingly. She had bright red ruby lipstick, which was what had attracted the killer to her. He had a love for all things red. "Guess we could spend our New Year giving the finger to God… Religion and religion, if you know what I mean…" The woman whispered suggestively, as she got closer to the killer. For the next two minutes, they were both whispering to each other. Neither Heller nor Cowper could make out what they were saying, but what they did know, was that the killer barely said any words at all. Cowper looked at his watch, it was 11:59PM. He thumped Heller and showed the watch, but Heller didn't care. He turned back to face the other two in the graveyard. Heller had never felt this nervous before in his entire life. After a few more moments, the killer reached into his kangaroo pockets. He deliberately dropped an envelope to the grassy ground beneath him. Then, in the dark black sky, the clouds were suddenly illuminated by a whining firework, raising into the sky and crackling. The woman turned with a smile to look, when without warning, the killer drew his knife. Heller had no time to shout out or do anything, as the killer

grabbed the woman's head and slashed her throat without any struggle. It all happened, literally, in a flash. Cowper froze. The woman began gurgling as blood spurted out from her wound, which the killer ducked to avoid. He grabbed her, after performing the injury within a second. "Greg!" Heller howled. The killer turned in surprise to the direction of Heller. He threw the woman, who fell headfirst onto a grave. The killer had only turned around to run out of the graveyard, when Heller jumped him. Cowper joined in quick succession. All three men grunted as they struggled.
"Drop the knife!" Cowper spat through his gritted teeth as he strenuously fought the killer. Heller bent the killer's arm backwards, and after a loud crack, the bloody knife fell to the ground. Heller then kicked the killer's right foot off the ground and threw him forward before grabbing once again. The killer was very injured, but made no noises other than grunting. He was towering over both detectives and was unbreakable in struggles, so it seemed. Heller tried his hardest to control the struggling killer on the ground. Sweat dripping from both their foreheads, now both Detectives were attempting to stop the killer from getting free.
"The handcuffs Greg, the handcuffs!" Heller yelled. Cowper lunged the handcuffs out of his coat pocket and after tossing and turning in sync with the killer, he further cracked the killer's arm, along with the other, to which the killer finally cried out in excruciating pain. Cowper finally got the handcuffs on the killer and tightened then so much so, that within seconds, the killer's hands were pale white.

"Got him!" Cowper announced. Both Detectives then brought the killer mercilessly to his knees. Heller did the honours of removing the hood. Below the hood, was messy and crazy quiffed hair, bouncing around. Cowper then took off the scarf that was wrapped around the mouth and nose. To their complete surprise, Heller and Cowper had unmasked the Midnight Murderer, as Jeffrey Stevens.

"Stevens...!" Cowper broke off in sheer shock.

Stevens was gasping for breath. "What... What the fuck? This isn't meant to be how it ends! I can't lose this game. I can't!"

Heller was staring at the still struggling Stevens with pure hatred. He wanted to kill him. Heller threw Stevens to the ground, before picking up the knife. Cowper stood in Heller's way.

"I told you I'd fucking have him! Now get out of my way Gregory."

"You can't James, you can't! You'll get thrown in prison!"

"Yeah, what fucking justice is that!? I'm gonna be his judge, jury and executioner, now get out of the way!"

"Don't throw your life away over a fucking scumbag like him James! Think about this!"

Heller then threw Cowper out of the way. Stevens was crawling towards the gate. Heller was about to pounce on his target, before he heard something behind him. He turned around, to see the woman lying with oozing blood on the grave she had fallen against. Heller dropped the knife. He then knelt down face to face with her.

"What's your name darling?" He asked softly.

The woman couldn't answer. Her eyes were barely open, she simply gazed lifelessly at Heller.
"We're going to get an ambulance here, okay? Your going to be alright." Heller threw Cowper his radio. "Get an ambulance here, right away!"
Cowper nodded and got up, joining Heller. Heller then had a dawning realisation. Stevens was long gone.
"Shit!" Heller got up. He saw that the gate was already open. "Stay with her!" Heller then dashed out of the chilling graveyard before Cowper could say or do anything. He simply stayed with the dying woman. She took one last gaze at him, before she began to close her eyes. She was giving up. Cowper, however, could still feel her pulse.

As the fireworks continued crackling and exploding in the night sky, a cuffed Stevens had already made his way towards the town centre. Having just easily ran down the steep Broadwater Bridge, a desperate Stevens was heading in random directions to try and lose Heller. Heller was not far behind. Stevens was not going to be escaping the clutches of James Heller. Stevens ran past a few curious and confused onlookers, even several house parties, throughout Newland Road and Chesswood Road. Stevens then passed suddenly onto Ladydell Road. However, for him, he had chosen the wrong side. He passed onto the side which was split in half by a train track. Beyond the tracks, was King Edward Avenue and Meredith Road. To him, these quiet roads were his refuge. Stevens got onto his back, and quickly slipped his arms onto his front. Getting back up, the speedy and physically fit Stevens began to climb the metal fence of Chesswood Junior School, intending to get onto the field. Stevens took a brisk glance behind him, hearing loud and impending footsteps. Heller dashed round the corner, and began to head for the fence. Stevens took a risk, and jumped onto the field. The field was so large and vast, that he couldn't see the other side of it in the concealed darkness. He then ran for the rest of the fence, which was on either side of the field. If he could get his luck right, Stevens could climb onto the tracks. If he used the overpass, which lead to the quieter neighbourhood beyond, it wouldn't have given him time to get away. As he got half way up the fence, Heller had already got onto the field. There was no time to lose, and Heller propelled himself onto the fence on the right of the field which Stevens was climbing. Heller tried to grab Stevens' foot, but missed, and Stevens jumped over the fence once again. Heller's coat got caught in the fence, somewhere. Stevens didn't have time to even get all smug with Heller, not even taunt him, like he usually did. Stevens got to his feet, unsteadily. He only had about 30 or 40 inches of track till he got to the final fence. Sighing in relief, Stevens stepped onto the track. Then, to his left, he could hear something distant. The distant sound, was heading straight for him. Stevens turned, to see the bright glow of the lights on the front of a train. In horror, Stevens tried to run across the track. Had he been quicker, he wouldn't have been harmed, but he was too slow. Heller watched on helplessly, as Stevens was knocked by the speeding train. Heller felt like the train had passed for weeks and weeks, before it had disappeared into the distance ahead. Heller got out his torch from his coat pocket, and shone it in the rough direction of Stevens. Heller saw the crumpled body of Stevens lying on the stones, just off the tracks.

Worthing Hospital was unusually quiet on the New Year. Heller had spent the first two hours of 2019 waiting outside an emergency room in the lonely hospital. He couldn't even see Stevens through the blinds. Cowper was waiting with him in the cold waiting room.
"And that's what happened. He got knocked by the train, not hit full on. But he's in critical condition." Heller then sat down beside Cowper. "What about the girl?"
"Her name was Hannah Emrys. She was 18. She died not long after you left."
Both men nodded in mournful silence. Neither of them said a word from then on. They both felt relieved though. Finally, the Midnight Murderer had been caught. Heller then noticed, after a long time, that something urgent was happening in the emergency room. It was in deep crisis. He rose, and was about to head to the room, when Green left the room. The Commissioner followed, and ignored Heller and Cowper.
"Well done James, Greg."
"What's going on in there?" Heller demanded.
Green rolled his eyes. Not in anger, but regret. It was almost fake regret. "Come with me James. Greg, you wait in the hallway."
Cowper nodded, perplexed, before leaving quickly.
Green then led Heller out of the waiting room, and into a dingy hallway outside. After a few moments, Green cleared his throat.

"So, what's going on?"
"Jeffrey Stevens has died, Heller. His body went into a severe cardiac arrest."
"I see. So, what now?"
Green took a prudent look at the surroundings, making sure nobody was present. He inhaled, composing himself to deliver further bad news.

Heller, disgusted, walked slowly in a trance out of the corridor and into the hallway. Cowper, who was waiting in the corridor, ran up to him desperately.
"So, what happened?"
Heller was silent. He looked tired. Simply, tired.
"Stevens died. But other than that. Nothing." He then wandered off further down the corridor, with a shocked Cowper following.
"What…!?" Cowper couldn't believe it.
Walking through the silent but intensely lit corridors, Heller was quiet for a few moments. He then stopped, near the reception of the hospital, when he turned to Cowper. Cowper noticed that Heller had very slightly teary eyes, but defeated eyes.
"Nothing's going to happen mate, nothing. Why should Sussex Police face the embarrassment of having already questioned a suspect several times? And arrested him, before he slipped through the net? As far as the world is gonna know, Jeffrey Stevens was killed by a train tonight, but has nothing to do with the murders. The killer got away…"

Cowper began to search for what to say. "Then... We just track the killer on CCTV, witness statements. Anything."

Heller shook his head. "Green's decided to cut funding to the case, completely, as of today. But he's going to keep the case open, to allow for more money to be pumped into it, which I'm sure he'll take before he leaves next month. We won't be allowed to use the resources to continue an investigation. The files will simply be put away along with the other millions, left to gather dust, leaving the case stamped as unsolved. Stevens lied about being blackmailed, he had Daines' phone. Not only that, but he didn't drive behind the killer the night Powell was killed, *he* was the driver of the car that she got in. He planted the knife on Hall that night we arrested him, in the pocket of his coat, and got his keys without him noticing on the night he killed Powell. He was cold, calculated, and clever. But as far as everyone else is concerned, he is innocent."

Cowper was feeling the fury rising throughout his body. He couldn't understand all this. "What? But we can't! We can't James!"

"We've got no choice. He and the Police and Crime Commissioner for Sussex Police have decided that the capture of the Midnight Murderer is a lost cause, it'll never happen. That's how everyone else will see it. They're gonna fake up the evidence and police testimonies from this evening."

"But he's guilty! He died, right here, officially under arrest."

Heller shrugged his shoulders. "He said nothing, nothing at all. That's enough to sweep it under the carpet. They'll

make out that he was also hunting for the killer too, wearing similar clothes… I mistook him for the killer, you get the general idea. Think of it Greg… The knock-on effect that this will have on the force!" Heller sarcastically tried to convince the angry Cowper. He then went back to his defeated and dejected state.
"We'll have to just tell people, tell the press!"
"It'll spread like wildfire, but simply as a conspiracy theory. Our little 15 minutes of fame."
"But he doesn't deserve the easy way out! He doesn't!"
Heller then smiled. "Then I should have killed him… Shouldn't I?"
Cowper's face dropped, in a horrifying realisation.
"Hmm?" Heller then inhaled. "Should have got him…" Heller admitted, before lifelessly and emptily leaving a similarly affected Cowper in the reception of the hospital. Cowper then slowly tagged along with his partner. With that, the Midnight Murders went unsolved, the case was cold.

Printed in Great Britain
by Amazon